Maybe Another Time

A Clean, Bittersweet Black Romance About Second Chances, Closure, and the Love That Lingers

(Steps Towards the Sun Book 2)

By

Seraphine Moonwater

Get bonus scenes, sneak peeks, deleted scenes and early access to the next book.

👉 👉 Tap here: https://subscribepage.io/f0S9zc

Or scan the QR code below:

DEDICATION

For the ones who rebuild their lives stitch by stitch,
Who carry their scars like compasses,
And find their way home—even when home is a
stranger.
For the mothers who hold the pieces,
The friends who light the path,
And every quiet heart that dares to beat again.
And for those who know that sometimes,
The bravest thing you can do is walk away.

TABLE OF CONTENTS

PRELUDE

The quiet in Vermont is different. It doesn't smother—it holds. It wraps itself around you like fresh snow, muffling the echoes of what you left behind. But even here, in this postcard-perfect town where smoke curls from chimneys and icicles glint like fractured glass, the past has a way of clawing through the frost.

Imara Hastings knows this better than anyone.

She arrived with a suitcase full of ghosts and a heart stitched shut. The betrayal that had chased her here—her best friend's laughter tangled with her boyfriend's lies—still hummed beneath her skin, a bitter refrain she couldn't unhear, no matter how hard she tried.

Nursing was supposed to be her escape, her purpose. But healing others was easier than healing yourself, and Vermont's icy beauty mirrors the walls she's built around her own cracked edges.

Yet this town, with its stubborn blizzards and salt-streaked roads, refuses to let her hide. In the relentless grip of winter, she collides with women who wear their scars like armor, patients who teach her the weight of resilience, and a man whose quiet steadiness threatens to melt the frost she's worked so hard to cultivate.

But healing is not a straight line. It's a stumble through snowbanks, a fight against the wind, a choice to thaw when every instinct screams to stay frozen.

This is a story about the ache of leaving, the terror of staying, and the fragile courage it takes to let new light into the wounds.

Because sometimes, the coldest places are where we finally learn to burn.

CHAPTER 1: THE ART OF UNRAVELING

The light, soft and apologetic like it knew I didn't want it there, snuck in through the curtains I used to love. My eyes cracked open, crusty and swollen, and for a moment, I thought I'd gone blind. No, worse—still alive.

Everything ached.

My chest felt like it was collapsing, my throat was raw, and my stomach churned. The image that looped in my mind was the only thing louder than my heartbeat.

Them. Together.

Tania's body wrapped around Derek's like she couldn't get close enough.

My Tania. My Derek.

I forced my legs over the side of the bed, ignoring the pull of the sheets that still smelled like the detergent my mom had been using since I was twelve. My room felt exactly like it did back then. Except now, the posters of girl groups long broken up made me cringe, and the stacks of boxes by the door screamed, "Failure."

I rubbed at my face, my fingers catching on the tear-sticky corner of my eye. A soft knock on the door broke the silence. My mom didn't wait for permission, of course. She stepped in, carrying a cup of tea in one hand and a plate of toast in the other.

"Mara...you should eat something," she said, her tone gentle but firm. The way only she could do, warm but impossible to argue with.

"I'm not hungry," I muttered, my voice hoarse.

"You're going to make yourself sick." She set the plate on my nightstand and looked at me like she could see straight through me. She probably could.

I looked away, picking at the hem of my pajama pants. My voice came out barely above a whisper. "Too late for that."

Her sigh was soft, but I felt it in my bones. She didn't push or argue; she just crossed her arms and leaned against the doorframe like she had all the time to wait me out.

"I'll leave it here," she said, nodding toward the toast and tea. "But, Imara, you need to start taking care of yourself. This wallowing isn't going to help."

"I'm trying," I lied because I didn't know what else to say. What does trying even look like when your whole world has imploded?

She didn't respond; she tilted her head like she was waiting for more. When I didn't offer anything, she gave a small nod. "Well, your dad and I are here if you need anything. Don't... don't hide yourself from us, sweetie."

"I'm no– I won't, Mom... thank you."

She sighed again before leaving the room, her footsteps soft but steady. The silence she left behind was deafening.

I glanced at the toast and tea, my stomach lurching at the thought of eating. Still, I forced myself to pick up the mug, letting the warmth seep into my hands. I took a small sip, the bitter taste grounding me just enough.

My phone sat face down on the dresser, a coward like me. It hadn't buzzed in hours, and I knew why. Nobody knew what to say to someone whose best friend and boyfriend decided to ruin their life in a single moment.

Even Jason and the rest of the crew had only sent the occasional check-in. I couldn't blame them—I hadn't answered. What would I even say?

"Hey, thanks for asking! I'm great. I'm just back in my childhood bedroom eating toast that tastes like cardboard and wondering if this pit in my stomach is my new permanent state. How are you?"

The thought made me snort and set the mug down harder than I'd meant to. The tea sloshed over the edge, staining the coaster below.

It didn't matter. Nothing felt like it mattered at that moment.

My dad's laugh echoed from the kitchen, deep and full like always, hitting me square in the chest. It's the kind of laugh that used to make me smile, even on my worst days, but now it just felt like a cruel reminder of how normal the world keeps spinning while mine came to a screeching halt.

I buried my face in my pillow, groaning into the fabric until the sound was muffled and raw.

A week. I'd spent an entire week holed up in this room, and tomorrow, the real world wouldn't let me hide anymore. The hospital had been patient, but I couldn't avoid going back. I'd already called in sick too many days in a row.

Tomorrow meant facing it all, especially Tania.

I screamed into my pillow again, harder this time, as if doing so would wring my anger out. But it didn't. It simmered under my skin, bubbling up whenever I thought about Tania and Derek.

Maybe I would just ignore her and bury myself in patient charts, rounds, and paperwork until the day ended. Maybe I could pretend she didn't exist. Pretend none of it happened.

The thought made my stomach twist, but I shoved it down and crawled under the blanket again, knowing it was pointless to keep running from the inevitable. The knot in my chest tightened as I drifted into a restless sleep, my mind replaying the scene repeatedly like a cruel, broken record.

The next morning, I dragged myself out of bed with all the enthusiasm of a zombie. I couldn't show up to work looking like I hadn't slept in weeks, even if it was true, so I shuffled over to the mirror and started dabbing concealer under my eyes.

A bit of mascara, a hint of blush, just enough to make me look like I've got it together.

By the time I had dressed and readied myself, my stomach was already doing backflips at the thought of stepping foot in that hospital again. The smell of coffee greeted me as I stepped into the kitchen. Mom stood by the stove, flipping pancakes, while Dad leaned close behind her and snuck a playful kiss on her cheek.

She swatted him away, laughing softly. They immediately noticed me and sprung apart like guilty teenagers caught in the act.

"We didn't see you there," Mom said, smoothing her apron.

I sighed, waving a hand dismissively. "You don't need to stop just because I'm here. Seriously. I'm fine."

Neither looked convinced, but I didn't give them a chance to argue. Grabbing my travel mug, I poured myself some coffee and headed out the door, trying not to let the lingering warmth of their moment follow me.

The drive to the hospital felt like it was on autopilot. My thoughts swirled, jumping from one regret to another. The years I poured into that relationship—years I'll never get back—flashed like a bad highlight reel.

Smiling through the exhaustion because I believed in his potential more than my own. I paid his tuition when he couldn't scrape it together, and I signed the lease on that overpriced apartment because it was his dream spot, not mine.

When I pulled into the parking lot, the pit in my stomach felt like it had grown claws. I cut the engine, gripping the steering wheel for a beat too long. Deep breath in, deep breath out. I glanced at my reflection in the rearview mirror and smoothed the concealer under my eyes. If you ignored the shadows and the tight set of my jaw, I might have looked presentable.

I tugged my bag out of the passenger seat with more force than necessary, the strap catching on the gear shift because it would. "Seriously?" I muttered, wrestling it free.

Slamming the door shut, I paused, taking a deep breath. My reflection in the car window stared back at me. "You've got this, Imara," I told myself with the kind of sarcasm that mad it clear I didn't believe a word. I slung the bag over my shoulder and started toward the hospital entrance.

The automatic doors hissed open, and the familiar smell of antiseptic and burnt coffee simmered. I kept my eyes straight ahead, focusing on the rhythm of my steps and the way my slip-ons scuffed against the tiles.

Straight to your station. Don't look left. Don't look right. Just—

"Morning, Imara!"

I glanced up just in time to catch Dr. Patel waving from the nurses' desk. I mustered a polite nod, forcing a smile that felt held together with duct tape and prayer. His expression flickered with something—sympathy, maybe pity—but he didn't push for conversation.

The break room was just up ahead. I didn't need to look to know who was inside—I could hear Tania. That laugh.

It stopped me cold, my grip tightening on the strap of my bag. My pulse quickened, my feet rooted to the spot even as my brain screamed at me to keep moving.

The room was just around the corner, the door half-open, and I didn't have to step inside to know she was there.

I eased forward, one step at a time, my heart hammering against my ribs. Through the gap in the doorway, I caught a glimpse of her—hair pulled back in that bun she always insisted on, hands wrapped around a coffee cup like she hadn't a care in the world.

She was talking to Kara, I think, one of the new junior nurses. As if hearing her name echoed in my mind, Kara glanced my way, and her smile faltered. Tania followed her gaze, and the color drained from her face when her eyes met mine.

Good.

Her grip tightened on the cup; her body stiffened just slightly before looking away like she could pretend she didn't see me or I didn't see her.

My chest felt tight, anger and hurt bubbling just beneath the surface, but I forced myself to keep walking.

I let the work take over—checked vitals, adjusted charts, and nodded politely at patients. It was all a blur, which was probably for the best. If I stopped long enough to think about it, I might have started replaying that look on her face. The one that almost made me believe she felt bad.

Almost.

When I got to Mr. Talbot's room, I was running on fumes, my good mood hanging by a thread and my tolerance for crankiness all but gone. He was sitting upright in bed, arms crossed so tight I half expected him to cut off his circulation. He'd pressed his lips into a thin line; a bad start already.

Mr. Talbot—my very own lesson in patience since two weeks ago—was exactly what you'd imagine when someone says "grumpy old man."

He was stubborn, rude, and perpetually annoyed, as if his hospital stay was a personal affront to his way of life.

The first time I met him, he called me a "glorified pill pusher" before I even had a chance to introduce myself. Since then, he'd kept up the streak—complaining about everything from the temperature of his soup to how I took his blood pressure. "Too tight," he'd bark. "Are you trying to strangle my arm?"

I plastered on my most diplomatic smile, preparing for whatever comment he was about to lob my way.

"Good afternoon, Mr. Talbot. How are we feeling today?"

He gave me the side-eye, his arms tightening over his chest. "What are you here to push on me this time?"

I ignored the bait, picking up the pill cup from the tray. "Just your medication. It'll help with—"

"Save the pep talk," he snapped, leaning back against the pillows. "Come in here with your clipboard and fake smile like you've figured it all out."

There it is.

"Mr. Talbot, you asked for my opinion last week, and I believe your exact words were, 'Don't sugarcoat it.' Which is it today?"

He narrowed his eyes. "Don't act like you care when you don't."

I froze, the pill cup hovering mid-air. "You know," I said slowly, my voice calm but dangerously close to cracking, "some of us do care, even if it doesn't meet your exacting standards. But tell me more about how I'm failing you."

He snorted like I'd just proven his point. "You're wasting your breath. I'm not some doe-eyed kid who believes in good intentions."

I set the pill cup down and met his gaze head-on. "Good, because I'm not here to convince you of anything. I'm here to help, whether you like it or not."

His mouth twitched, and I almost mistook it for a concession. But then he smirked—that smug, maddening smirk made me want to chuck the pill cup out the window.

"Please. You're here because you've got nothing else going for you. Just like everyone else who comes in here pretending to care. But I'll credit you for one thing—you've got guts, showing your face when half the staff is probably laughing behind your back."

I forced myself to stand still, planting my feet firmly like I could stop the wave from crashing over me. "I don't know what you're talking about." The words came out so quickly that I could feel the lie before I'd even finished speaking.

He tilted his head, his smirk widening. "Oh, sure you don't. Word travels fast around here, you know. Poor little nurse gets cheated on by her man and her best friend. Guess they didn't think much of you either, huh?"

Heat bloomed under my collar, raced to my neck, and pooled in my cheeks. My face felt like it was on fire, and I couldn't stop it—not the flush, not the way my jaw tightened so hard it ached. My stomach twisted, the kind of knot that starts low and drags everything down with it.

"Wow. You must be so proud of yourself. Picking at someone's pain because you've nothing else going on."

He shrugged, completely unbothered. "Call it as I see it. At least I'm honest. Can't say the same for your so-called friends, though."

It was like a rubber band snapped in my brain. My shoulders stiffened, my spine grew rigid, and my jaw clenched so tightly that it popped. "You know what, Mr.

Talbot?" I set the pill cup down harder than I meant to. "You're right—I've got my mess to deal with. But at least I'm trying. What's your excuse? Huh? You sit here, day after day, pushing away everyone who tries to help you. Maybe that's why you're alone. Not because you're sick, but because you've made yourself impossible to care about."

His smirk faltered momentarily, and I felt the tiniest pang of regret—not because I didn't mean it, but because I let him drag me to his level. "Take your pills, Mr. Talbot. It's important for your recovery."

He glared at me but picked up the pill cup without another word. I couldn't wait for thanks. I was out the door before he'd swallowed.

The moment my station door clicked shut behind me, I immediately sagged against the wall, the clipboard slipping from my hands. My chest felt tight; my breaths were shallow. I pressed the heels of my hands against my eyes, trying to block out the sting of tears.

I didn't lose my cool. Not with patients, not with anyone. But hearing him throw my humiliation back at me like that? It's what everyone must be saying.

I pulled out my phone, hoping for anything to distract me, but the notification on the screen made my stomach drop: Missed Call: Charlene.

Before I could even process it, another buzz—a voicemail. My thumb hovered over the play button, dread pooling in my gut as I pressed it.

"Imara, it's Charlene. I've left a few messages now, but the rent's overdue. Your name's still on the lease, and if I don't receive a payment by the end of the week, I'll have no choice but to take legal action."

I closed my eyes, inhaling slowly through my nose. Rent for the apartment I hadn't set foot in since the day I packed up and left Derek's sorry ass to his excuses.

I tapped on his name, and there were mountains of unanswered messages. The screen flooded with blue bubbles, his voice in text form, desperate in some, casual in others. The early ones, which had come in just days after I left, were dripping with apology: "I'm sorry, babe, please just let me explain." "You don't have to talk to me, but at least read this." "I messed up. I know I messed up. Just give me one more chance."

It was almost pathetic, but it didn't last. By week two, the tone shifted. He stopped apologizing and stopped trying. A message made my stomach twist: "Guess you don't care. Fine. I'm done."

Done. Like he gave up after a week of barely trying, as if that's all the effort I was worth to him. My fingers hovered over the screen, and a bitter laugh caught in my throat. It was funny how someone could treat you like an afterthought and still expect you to clean up after them.

I scrolled past the unread messages, refusing to give them more attention than they deserved. They were part of the past—messy, ugly, and staying exactly where I left them. Right now, I needed to focus on damage control. My credit wasn't waiting for Derek to find his moral compass.

Imara: *"Derek, the landlord called. The rent hasn't been—"*

I stopped, erasing the sentence with a frustrated swipe of my thumb. Too direct. He'll take it as an attack and twist the whole thing back on me. I groaned, biting the edge of my thumbnail as I tried to think.

With a deep breath, I picked up the phone and started again.

Imara: *"Good afternoon, Derek; the landlord called. The rent hasn't been paid, and my name is still on the lease. You need to—"*

I paused again, my thumb hovering over the delete button. My chest tightened as I stared at the screen. If I soften it, he'll take it as a weakness. If I'm too firm, he'll fight me on it.

Imara: *"Derek, the landlord, called. The rent hasn't been paid, and my name is still on the lease. You need to decide what you're going to do. You have two options: either take over the lease and deal with Charlene or move out so I can terminate it. Those are your only choices. Let me know by the end of the day."*

I reread the message, my heart pounding as I analyzed every word. Is it too harsh? Is that not harsh enough? I erased "deal with Charlene" and replaced it with "work with the landlord," only to change it again. I was writing to a stranger instead of someone I spent years with.

I dropped the phone onto the counter, groaning into my hands. For a fleeting moment, the idea of paying the rent and pretending he didn't exist felt so much easier. But that's how he always won: by making me feel like dealing with him wasn't worth the effort.

I picked up the phone and glared at the screen, determined now. "No more second chances," I muttered as I hit send. The message whooshed out, final and unchangeable.

I stared at the chat momentarily before locking the phone and shoving it into my pocket. My hands trembled as I pressed them flat against the counter, grounding myself. I'd done my part. The ball was in his court now.

For once, I hoped he'd surprise me—but I was not holding my breath.

CHAPTER 2: TO THE BACKSEAT

The front door creaked as I stepped inside. My shoes felt fused to my feet, and my scrubs felt like sandpaper against my body. The faint aroma of something stewing on the stove greeted me.

"In the kitchen!" my dad's voice called out before I could close the door.

I hesitated, torn between slipping straight to my room and facing the inevitable concern I knew would be written all over their faces. With a sigh, I trudged toward the kitchen, my bag slung over my shoulder like dead weight.

"Hey, sweetheart," my mom said, glancing up from the pot she was stirring. Her eyes narrowed as she took in my slouched posture and the dark circles I didn't even bother to cover today. "Today didn't go as easily as I'd hoped, huh?"

"Something like that," I muttered, setting my bag down by the door.

My dad looked up from the newspaper he was reading at the table, his forehead creasing. "Were your friends not excited to see you?"

I shrugged, not trusting myself enough to speak without spilling everything: Mr. Talbot, Tania. My throat tightened just thinking about it.

"Have you eaten?" my mom asked.

"I'm fine," I said quickly, waving her off. "I'm just gonna head to my room."

"Wait, we're going to the Martins' barbecue tonight. You should come."

The Martins are an older couple who threw every kind of neighborhood party, from Fourth of July cookouts to random "because it's Friday" dinners.

Their barbecues were always big, loud, and full of people who made it their mission to know everyone else's business.

"No, thanks." The words were out of my mouth before she even finished. "I'm exhausted. I just want to sleep."

"You've been doing nothing but working and hiding in your room," she pressed, setting the spoon down with a sharp clink. "You need to get out and be around people. It'll do you good."

"Mom, seriously, I'm not in the mood—"

"You're coming," she said firmly, her hands on her hips. "It's not up for discussion."

My dad looked between us, but he didn't intervene. He knew better than to get in the middle of one of Mom's decisions.

I stared at her, willing her to back down, but she didn't budge. Finally, I let out a heavy sigh. "Fine."

"Good." She nodded, satisfied, and turned back to the stove. "This stew will be lunch for tomorrow."

I dragged myself to my room and threw my bag onto the chair in the corner before flopping onto the bed. The thought of facing a crowd of cheerful people made my stomach churn, but arguing with my mom was like trying to use a whisper to stop a train.

For a few minutes, I just lay there, staring at the ceiling and listening to the faint sounds of my parents in the kitchen, the clink of dishes, the low hum of their voices, and the occasional burst of my dad's laugh.

I quickly changed into jeans and a yellow spaghetti-string top.

A knock at the door startled me. "We're leaving in ten," my mom said through the wood.

"Great," I muttered, dragging myself upright.

I glanced in the mirror on my dresser, grimacing at my reflection. My hair was messy, my eyes were bloodshot, and my skin looked dull. I tried to flatten some of the standing strands from my pixie cut, not even bothering to check if it looked decent.

When I left my room, my parents were by the door, jackets in hand. My mom gave me a quick once-over, her lips tightening, but she said nothing. My dad opened the door, gesturing for me to step out first.

As we piled into the car, I leaned against the window, the cool glass soothing my temple.

By the time we pulled up to the Martins' house to the sound of laughter and music spilling out into the street, I was already counting down the minutes until I could leave.

The Martins' backyard was picture-perfect, the kind that could grace the cover of a lifestyle magazine.

String lights crisscrossed above, and a long buffet table groaned under the weight of barbecue staples—burgers, hot dogs, baked beans, and more desserts than anyone could eat.

I followed my parents through the crowd, keeping my head down as much as possible.

People were everywhere, gathered in groups around the patio furniture, lounging by the firepit, and standing in clusters with drinks in hand. Laughter bubbled through the air, loud and unrelenting, as though it was mocking me.

"Imara, you made it!" Mrs. Martins swooped in before I could dodge her, her perfume hitting me first. She hugged me tight, the sequins on her blouse scratched against my cheek. "Sweetheart, it's been too long. How are you holding up?"

"Fine, thank you, Mrs. Martin," I said, forcing a smile that felt like it might crack my face.

She leaned back, her hands gripping my shoulders as she searched my expression. Pity was all over her face. "Well, you're looking good, at least. That Derek... never deserved you anyway."

"Absolutely," Mrs. Jackson chimed in, her red lipstick so bright it made her teeth glow. "I was just telling your mom how proud we are of you for staying so strong."

I nodded, my throat too tight to speak.

"Thank you," I murmured, glancing past her for a way out.

"And you know, dear," she continued, leaning in like she was about to share a secret, "Everyone always thought you were too good for him. You're going to come out of this better than ever."

The words were meant to comfort me but only made my stomach churn. I muttered something polite and slipped away, ducking past a group of kids chasing each other with sparklers.

As I moved through the yard, the whispers and stares followed me. Some were subtle—glances from the corner of their eyes. Others were bold, their pity thick enough to suffocate me. I caught bits of conversation floating on the warm evening air.

"Poor girl. I don't know how she's even holding it together." "I knew Derek wasn't good enough for her." "I heard he was with her best friend, of all people."

I gripped the edge of a nearby table, my fingers curling around the smooth surface as I tried to steady myself. It's like they thought their pity would somehow make things better. It didn't.

By the time I reached the far edge of the yard, my pulse was thrumming in my ears. I leaned against the deck's railing, gripping it like the only thing keeping me upright.

The cheerful noise of the barbecue felt like nails on a chalkboard, and I couldn't stop the spiral of thoughts in my head.

Why did I let my mom talk me into this?

My gaze fell on a pile of mismatched chairs in the corner of the yard, stacked haphazardly and half-forgotten.

"Imara, dear?" Mrs. Martin's voice rang out again, but I didn't turn. I pushed off the railing, making my way toward the house. Maybe I could breathe if I could just make it to the bathroom or some quiet corner.

I retreated to the car, shoulders hunched as I sunk into the seat and closed the door behind me.

The muffled chatter from the barbecue faded into the background, replaced by the quiet hum of the engine as I twisted the keys to the accessory position.

I leaned back against the seat, stared up at the ceiling, and let out a shaky breath.

The first tear fell before I could stop it, rolling hot and fast down my cheek. I swiped at it, then another, and another, until I finally gave up, letting them fall freely.

The tight knot in my chest loosened just enough for me to feel everything—my broken heart, the stares, the pitying comments, and worst of all, the crushing sense of failure.

Twenty minutes later, I caught sight of my parents through the window. My mom was holding a couple of foil-covered dishes, her lips pressed into a thin line. My dad trailed behind her, shaking his head slightly, a guilty frown etched across his face.

They both climbed into the car, the scent of barbecue filling the small space as my mom settled the dishes on her lap.

"We didn't stay too long, did we?" my dad asked, glancing at me in the rearview mirror.

"No," I managed, forcing my lips into something resembling a smile. "It's fine. You guys could've even stayed longer. I-I'm fine."

My mom sighed, her fingers fiddling with the edge of one of the foil covers. "We just... we thought maybe being around people would help. You've been so..." Her voice trailed off, but I knew the unspoken word: broken.

Tears sprung to my eyes again, and I quickly looked out the window, willing them not to fall. My voice was barely a whisper. "I'm okay. I just need more time."

They exchanged glances, and my dad's hand found my mom's on the console. "We hate seeing you like this, sweetheart," he said softly.

His words cracked something inside me, and I blinked furiously, biting my bottom lip until it stung. "I'm sorry," I choked out. "I don't mean to—"

"You don't have to apologize," my mom cut in. She twisted in her seat, holding something out toward me. A honey bun, still wrapped, the kind I've loved since I was a kid.

My throat tightened as I took it from her, fingers trembling. "Thanks," I muttered, my voice rough.

"You've been through a lot," she continued, her expression softening. "No one expects you to bounce back overnight."

My dad reached back and squeezed my knee. "We're here, kiddo. However long it takes."

I nodded, unable to trust my voice, and they didn't press me further.

When we got home, we all climbed out of the car together. My dad stretched, groaning quietly, and my mom carried the dishes inside. Before I could follow, my dad hugged me, his arms warm and steady.

"Love you, Imara," he said.

"Love you too, Dad."

My mom stepped back onto the porch and frowned at the two of us. "Don't let the food get cold," she said, but the corner of her mouth twitched as she held back a smile.

I felt their love and unwavering support, even if I hated that my sadness was rubbing off on them. I hated being the emotional burden Derek practically accused me of being.

Either way, I let them guide me inside, my dad's hand on my shoulder and my mom muttering about heating the macaroni.

CHAPTER 3: MAPS IN THE DELUGE

I pushed through the office doors, thermos clutched in one hand, the faint aroma of cinnamon and honey wafting from the oats inside. Mom had been smuggling care into my routine—oats, tea, a kiss on the forehead before I left.

I took a sip, the warm sweetness coating my tongue, and even though my stomach still churned from everything, I let myself appreciate it for a second.

A very short second.

The exhaustion hit me before I even made it halfway across the room. My body was here, but my mind was dragging its feet like a kid on their way to detention.

"Morning, Imara." The receptionist barely glanced up as she handed me a clipboard. I managed a half-smile that probably looked like a grimace, murmuring a quick "Morning."

I tucked my bag into the staff locker and headed toward my station, sipping slowly as I walked.

My station came into view, and my chest tightened at seeing an open chart. Of course. I left it unfinished before bailing last week. I sucked my teeth quietly, annoyed at myself.

I dropped my bag onto the chair, already calculating how much of my break this mess would eat into, when something tugged at my attention. The corner of my eye caught scuffed white Skechers peeking out from under the desk across the hall. My steps faltered.

The tightness in my chest spread, sinking lower as my gaze lifted. Arms crossed, shoulders stiff. Tania was looking everywhere but at me, her eyes darting toward the hallway, the window, her hands—anywhere but here.

I gripped the edge of the desk, willing the air around me to hold steady. I couldn't shake the hollow sadness taking over, the kind that settles in when you realize there's no fixing this.

"Imara, we need to talk."

The words barely landed before heat rose in my chest, spreading to my face, jaw, and hands, tightening against the desk. I stood there, rooted in place, glaring at her with every ounce of anger I'd swallowed for the past week.

Her shoulders slumped ever so faintly. She looked down at her feet, at those same damn shoes, and for a brief moment, I wondered if she felt as stupid as I did.

I froze, my hand tightening on the thermos. My pulse quickened, but I forced my face to stay neutral. "Move," I said flatly, stepping toward the door.

"No, I'm serious. We need to talk," Tania repeated, her voice a little more desperate now.

"Do you think there's something left to say?" I asked.

Her mouth opened, but no sound came out. She looked down, shifting uncomfortably on her feet. "I know I messed up, okay? What I did was—"

"Don't," I snapped, cutting her off. "Don't stand here and give me some empty apology, Tania. Don't insult me like that."

She flinched. "It wasn't supposed to happen like this. I didn't mean for any of this, honestly. You know I'd never intentionally hurt you."

"Oh, spare me." I laughed bitterly. "You didn't mean to sleep with my boyfriend? You didn't mean to betray your best friend? Please enlighten me. What did you mean to do?"

Her face crumpled. "A-A few months back, I went to his place to talk to him. I wanted him to know how much he was hurting you—how wrong he was for everything he'd done."

"You went to lecture him about being a terrible boyfriend and ended up what? Comforting him? Falling into bed with him?"

"It wasn't like that." She stepped forward. "He started talking, and Derek has this way of twisting things. You know that."

"And yet you still believed him."

"I hated myself for what happened, Imara. I still do. But—"

"But?" I interrupted.

She shook her head, her voice breaking. "Look, I'm not trying to justify anything. I just—"

"Wait... wait... Are you... are you still seeing him?"

She froze, and her eyes widened for just a second too long before she glanced away.

"Oh my— You're still with him. Aren't you?"

"Imara—"

"You are," I said, the realization crashing over me like a wave. "You're still with him. After everything."

"It's complicated," she whispered, her voice cracking.

"Wow." I managed to mutter. That's all I really could say.

She pressed her lips together, and for a moment, I saw it: the guilt, the regret, the tiny, pathetic part of her that knew how wrong this was.

"You told me to leave him... You told me he was no good. That I deserved better, and all that time, you were just waiting for your turn."

"That's not true!" she said, stepping forward, her voice desperate. "I wanted you to leave because I knew what he was doing. I knew he didn't deserve you."

"And yet here you are," I said, trembling with rage. "With him. How can you even stand there and pretend you care about me?"

"I'm sorry," she whispered, holding her hands helplessly.

"No need to be... Enjoy your new life, Tania. I wish you all the best with the man who cheated on me with you."

Without another word, I turned and walked away, my chest tight, my hands trembling. I didn't look back. I couldn't. If I did, I might not be able to keep walking.

I tucked my clipboard under my arm and headed down the hall, doing my best to shove the swirling mess of hurt and anger into some dusty corner of my mind where it could stay until I could get the time—or courage—to deal with it.

Which probably means it would sit there forever. Out of sight, out of mind, right? At least, that was the plan.

When I opened Mrs. Grayson's door, her voice reached me before I could look up.

"You look like someone stole your last Ferrero Rocher."

Despite the hot blood pumping through my veins, I could hardly stop the snicker that left my mouth.

"In that case, you look much better than me. How are you feeling?"

Mrs. Grayson had been at the hospital for weeks now, working her way through post-op recovery like a champ. And by "champ," I mean a stubborn firecracker of a woman who claimed she didn't have time to be sick. Her charm was the kind that snuck up on you—like the way she insisted on pronouncing "antibiotics" as "anti-bi-yotics" or how she hoarded chocolates in her nightstand for when "hospital food gets too depressing."

She sighed deeply, tilting her head to the side as a slither of a smile crawled on her lips. She'd brushed her silver hair neatly, and her cheeks looked a little rosier today.

"I do feel better. I managed to keep most of the food down for a whole week," she said, lifting her hands like she'd scored a touchdown. "I admit— and please don't judge me, but I haven't taken one of those awful pills for three days."

I groaned loudly, knowing I would have to report this. "Mrs. Grayson, those antibiotics are really important for your infect—"

"I know, I know," she grumbled, "But I told you, my body's tougher than it looks. Those pills make me feel like a tractor has run me over."

I pulled up a stool next to her, pursing my lips together. "Look, you've been doing the work, and it shows. But you need to follow the doctor's orders to a T. We can't have anything going wrong—you can't like me that much that you'd want to stay longer here."

She patted her bed, motioning for me to sit closer. "Fine. I know I've been raising hell here. I'll do better—I'll take those nasty pills."

"Perfect, that's all I ask. Now, I have about five minutes—what gossip do you have for me?"

With a start, she launched into updates about her life—the new book her daughter brought her, a recipe she wanted to try once she was home, and a knitting project that sounded more like a war zone than a hobby.

When it was time to leave, she patted my hand and gave me a look that went straight to my heart.

"You're a good one, you know that? I don't know what's got your shoulders sitting so heavy—or why I haven't seen you in an entire week." She gave me a knowing look, and I'm grateful she didn't bring it up first. "But don't let the world chew you up, sweetheart. So many of us appreciate you."

"You never fail to butter me up... but that won't get you out of those antibiotics."

"Darn it!" I squeezed her hand before stepping out of the room, and I'd long forgotten all about Tania and her apology.

By the time the shift winded down, I was running on fumes. My body felt like it had been wrung out and left to dry, and my brain was in no better shape. I made my way to the lobby, bag slung over one shoulder, only for a torrential downpour to greet me.

With a heavy breath, I leaned against the wall near the glass doors, watching sheets of rain soak the parking lot.

My car felt like it was miles away. I groaned quietly, pressing my forehead against the cool glass. This day just won't end.

"You look like you could use a drink—or a vacation. Maybe both, actually—a drink on vacation."

I turned to see Nurse Beattie, one of the senior nurses on the board, standing a few feet away with an umbrella in her hand. She was always so put together—her scrubs somehow wrinkle-free, her white sneakers spotless even after a 12-hour shift.

She'd tucked the umbrella neatly under her arm like she was a walking advertisement for composure, which only made me feel more like a mess.

"I won't argue with that," I replied, the words tumbling out before I could stop them. My tone was too dry to pass for a joke.

Beattie chuckled softly, taking a step closer. "Rough day?"

"Something like that," I muttered, rubbing my arms. "I'd settle for being somewhere with no Derek or Tania within a hundred-mile radius."

The words slipped out before I could catch them, and I immediately regretted it. When she didn't reply right away, I glanced at her, and sure enough, she was giving me the kind of look you give a fragile thing you're scared to touch. I hate it.

"You ever think about it?" she asked after a pause.

For a split second, I was ready to snap—ready to launch into a tirade about how, yes, I thought about Tania and Derek every second of every day, about how their betrayal felt. It was carved into my chest and impossible to ignore, no matter how hard I tried. But before I could say anything, she clarified, her tone softer now.

"A change of scenery, I mean," she said, shifting her umbrella to her other hand. "We've got that relocation program for travel nurses, you know. Could be a fresh start."

She said it casually, but how her eyes lingered on me felt anything but. Beattie had a knack for reading people— probably why she was on the board—and right now, I felt like she was peeling back every layer I'd been trying to keep together.

I blinked, caught off guard. "I... no, not really."

I raised an eyebrow, surprised. "Relocation program? Is that different from the travel nurse program?"

Beattie tilted her head, a faint smile playing on her lips. "A little. It's more permanent than bouncing from state to state every few months. This is about putting down roots somewhere new—transferring to a hospital in a different city or state and staying there."

"Huh. I didn't even know that was an option."

"Well, you've been on pause with the travel program, haven't you?"

I nodded slowly, my throat tightening. "Yeah. I asked for a break after... everything." My voice faltered, and I didn't have to say more. Beattie didn't press.

She shifted her umbrella to her other hand and placed her free hand on her hip. "You look burned out, Imara. You haven't been here long enough to allow this place— and whatever else, to do that to you. Maybe it's time to take care of yourself for a change. You can't fix everything, Imara."

I snorted softly, the sound more bitter than amused. "Easier said than done, don't you think?"

"Maybe. But you've got options. Don't forget that."

"Options," I echoed under my breath. I glanced at the rain streaking down the glass, watching the droplets race each other to the bottom. There was a strange warmth spreading in my chest.

"Just something to think about," she said. Headlights sliced through the rain, and she gave me a small, knowing smile. "Take care of yourself, Imara. No one else is gonna do it for you."

I nodded, unable to muster anything more than a quiet "Thanks" as she turned and walked toward the waiting car, her umbrella shielding her from the storm. I watched her momentarily, my thoughts swirling, and then glanced back at the rain-soaked lot ahead of me.

Options.

The idea lingered as I turned back to the rain. Could I just leave?

It felt absurd, laughable even. My entire life was here—my parents, my childhood memories, the good ones and the bad.

Derek's face flashed in my mind, uninvited. Even with all the heartbreak tied to this town, it felt like leaving would be running away. It would mean abandoning the parts of me tangled up in these streets, the people I cared about, the life I'd spent years building.

What life? My mind whispered back to me.

The wind picked up, whipping my hair against my forehead and sending droplets straight into my eyes. I finally mustered the courage to sprint through the rain to my car.

It stung—my hair product mixing with the rain, burning like hell—but I pushed it back and squinted through the downpour. My car felt miles away, parked at the far end of the lot, a good hundred yards that might as well be a mile in this weather.

The first few steps were miserable. The rain fell in sheets, soaking my clothes to the skin in seconds. My scrubs stuck to me, heavy and clammy, and my socks squelched with every step as puddles splashed up against my calves. I cursed everything—this day, this storm, the distance between me and my car.

I can't remember at what point it starts to feel... different.

My heart pounded harder, not just from the sprint but the rush—the rain, the cold, the wildness. My chest heaved, and I couldn't tell if I was laughing or just gasping for air, but I let it happen. The rain streamed down my face, dripping from my chin, and the burn in my eyes made me laugh harder. It was ridiculous. I must have looked insane—soaked to the bone, half-blind, with my hair plastered to my forehead like some rom-com cliché.

Options. That's what Beattie said. I've got options. I was not stuck here. Even if it made me feel guilty and meant leaving behind pieces of myself, the idea that I could walk away and choose something else flooded me with the same adrenaline as the run.

When I reached my car, I was shaking from the cold, my socks squelching with every move, and water dripping off me in streams. I fumbled with my keys, shoved them into the lock, and yanked the door open. Collapsing into the driver's seat, I slammed the door shut against the storm, my breath coming in ragged bursts.

The rain drummed against the roof, and I just sat there laughing like a madwoman, water pooling beneath me. My heart was still racing, my body trembling, but I felt alive for the first time in what felt like forever. Fully, undeniably alive.

CHAPTER 4: CATERED COLLISIONS

On Saturday morning, I sat on the edge of my bed, staring at the half-unpacked boxes littering my room.

My mom had been dropping not-so-subtle hints all week about how they were taking up space and how I needed to "settle in." I get it—it was her polite way of saying, You're not a guest here anymore, so act like it.

I pulled the first box closer, slicing through the packing tape with an old pair of scissors that barely did the job. Inside, a pile of clothes greeted me—sweaters that still smelled faintly of lavender detergent and summer dresses I never got to wear.

I picked up a cream-colored cardigan, the soft fabric slipping through my fingers for a second; it was just a cardigan. But it was not. It was the dinner date—last fall, overpriced pasta, and Derek trying too hard to convince me that the restaurant's three-dollar breadsticks were "authentic." I tossed it aside, shaking my head.

Next, my fingers found something silky: a blue sundress. Oh, this one was special. The dress I bought for the beach weekend Derek insisted on planning. I never wore it. I never got to because, by that time, he had changed his mind about going out with me anymore.

How did I not see the signs?

Before I could torture myself with another wave of nostalgia, my hand drifted to my phone, unlocking it almost without thinking. My thumb hovered over the screen, and there it was—the text I sent Derek about the rent. Still unread. Still unanswered.

I scoffed, the sound sharp and bitter. Of course. Typical.

With more force than necessary, I tossed my phone back onto the bed, where it bounced once before settling against the rumpled sheets. My gaze snapped back to the pile of clothes, and suddenly, the fabric looked less like memories and more like taunts.

"Figures," I muttered, yanking another sweater and tossing it onto the pile. "Can't handle rent, can't handle a relationship. At least he's dependable—in all the worst ways."

The relocation program buzzed quietly at the back of my mind as I folded shirts and stacked jeans in neat piles.

I folded a shirt, smoothing the wrinkles, but my hands moved on autopilot. My mind drifted, unbidden, to Beattie's words. Options. That tiny, harmless little word had somehow lodged into my brain and refused to leave.

I pictured her standing there with her umbrella, telling me to care for myself like it was the most obvious thing in the world. The thought stirred something deep in my chest, and before I could stop it, I was replaying the way I felt sprinting through the rain—wild and soaked, every muscle burning but alive. Sigh, it had felt good doing something completely unlike me.

Running through that storm had felt like a rebellion, like grabbing the reins and steering myself away from all the... heaviness.

I swallowed hard, shaking my head as I folded another blouse and stacked it on the growing pile. Moving to another state would be just as crazy, wouldn't it? Packing up and starting fresh somewhere far away—leaving behind the mess, the whispers, and the people keeping me in place.

My heart skipped, a tiny flicker of adrenaline sparking in my chest at the thought. Somewhere, I was not the girl everyone whispered about, not the one cleaning up Derek's messes or dodging Tania's shadow...just me, carving out something new.

Stop. No. You're not doing that.

My parents would kill me. Moving away now? After they'd opened their doors to me and practically babied me back to normalcy? After everything?

I closed the box flaps a little too hard, letting out a frustrated sigh. Running away wasn't the answer. I was not some reckless teenager who could just blow up her life because it felt good for five minutes. Traveling and returning for a few weeks is one thing, but relocating for months and months is another. My family was here. And whether I liked it or not, my responsibilities were here, too.

I pushed the thought to the back of my mind, locking it away with all the other things I didn't have time to think about. Beattie's voice faded, the word options dissolving faintly in the background.

When I'd emptied the rest of the boxes, my room looked a little more like mine again. I draped a throw blanket over the back of the chair by the window and tucked some books onto the shelf.

I sifted through the contents, pulling out a framed picture of my parents and me on my high school graduation day. My dad's grin was as wide as the horizon, and my mom looked like she was mentally planning my college dorm setup even as she smiled for the camera. My younger self stood between them, bright-eyed and hopeful.

I had no idea.

"Imara, honey!" my mom's voice called from downstairs, cutting through my thoughts. "Do you mind picking up some food we ordered? Your dad's got a bit of back pain. It should be ready by now!"

It's Saturday, which meant the kitchen was officially closed. My parents didn't cook on Saturdays. It was part of their unofficial but very serious marital truce. I almost heard my dad saying, "Why argue over whose turn it is when we can argue over what to order instead?"

"Yeah, I'll get it!" I shouted back, setting the picture frame on my nightstand. I slipped on my shoes and grabbed my keys, glad for the excuse to get out of the house for a bit.

The smell of Fried chicken, buttery rolls, something sweet baking in the back—the scent made you want to forget whatever diet you pretended to be on— hit me like a warm hug the second I stepped into Cater 2 You.

The place was cozy; the wooden accents and chalkboard menus had just the right amount of fancy handwriting to let you know they meant business.

I'd driven past this place more times than I can count, always thinking, I'll stop in next time. But "next time" never came. Life got busy. Budgets got tight, especially when you were carrying your ex-boyfriend's entire financial life on your back.

I stepped up to the counter, glancing at the baskets of cookies and muffins wrapped in plastic—tempting little traps I already knew I would not leave without one. The cashier, a bright-eyed young woman with braids pulled back into a bun, greeted me with a smile.

"Hi, I'm picking up for Hastings?" I said, leaning on the counter.

"Got it! One sec," she chirped before disappearing into the back.

I pulled out my phone, and my thumb was already swiping through the notifications out of habit. Charlene hadn't sent a follow-up yet, which should have felt like sweet relief. But it didn't—not really. The silence just gave my anxiety room to stretch and settle deeper into my chest. I blew a slow, shaky breath, letting my shoulders drop slightly.

To distract myself, I glanced around the shop again, taking in the little details: the mason jars of flowers, the soft hum of conversation from the tables, the comforting warmth of the place. My gaze drifted toward the corner by the window, where someone familiar-looking stood with their back to me, phone pressed to their ear.

I squinted, tilting my head slightly, the familiarity tugging at the edges of my mind like a fraying thread. Then he turned slightly, enough for me to catch his profile, and my stomach dropped.

I glanced over my shoulder, more out of reflex than curiosity, and my stomach twisted into a knot.

For a second, everything slowed. My breath caught in my throat, my pulse pounding in my ears so loudly I couldn't hear anything else. All the blood drained from my body, leaving me cold and weightless, as if I might float right out of my skin.

I blinked, hoping I was imagining it, but when I looked again, he was still there—tall, with that same confident stance, phone in one hand, gesturing slightly with the other.

It's him. It was him.

My heart slammed against my ribs, the panic rising so quickly it made me dizzy. What are the chances? Of all the places, on all the days, Derek would be here. Right now.

I gripped the counter's edge to steady myself, my knuckles whitening as I willed my body to stop reacting. He hadn't noticed me yet—he was too busy with his phone call, his attention entirely elsewhere. But I couldn't move, couldn't think. My mind raced, every worst-case scenario playing out in vivid detail.

Do I leave? Do I stay? The cashier could come back any second; the last thing I wanted was a scene. But my legs felt like lead; all I could manage to do was stand there, frozen.

As if he sensed my gaze burning into the back of his head, Derek turned. His eyes widened when they met mine, but not with guilt or regret—just plain surprise, as if he'd run into an old friend at the grocery store. He even smiled. Smiles.

Before I could think or move, he walked toward me, sliding his phone into his pocket, his stride casual and unbothered. That same easy charm I used to fall for was still there, wrapped around him like a perfectly tailored coat. He stopped a few feet away, close enough that I could smell his cologne—clean, sharp, and probably new.

"Imara," he said as if this was the happiest coincidence in the world. "Hey. Wow, it's been a while."

My throat tightened, words tangling up before they could form. I blinked at him, my brain struggling to process what was happening. "Yeah," I managed, my voice quieter than I wanted it to be. "It has."

He shifted his weight, his smile growing wider. "I got your message," he said as if this is the kind of thing he does all the time, as if it's not a text about rent that he ignored for days. "Sorry I didn't respond—I've just been extra busy these past few days. You know how it is."

Busy. He's been busy.

My stomach twisted; for a moment, I could only stare at him. He looked polished. His clothes were neat, as if someone had pressed them with care. He had a fresh haircut, and his shoes were spotless and polished to a shine. There was no wrinkle, scuff, or sign of the man I left behind.

"I handled everything with Charlene, so she shouldn't bother you now," he continued, and my eyebrows immediately raised into my forehead. He chuckled. "You don't have to worry. I got a job, and I can take care of it now. It's all good."

He got a job just like that.

After years of me begging him and pleading with him to step up and take some of the weight off my shoulders, he suddenly decided to be responsible now when I was no longer part of the equation.

"I hope you're doing well," he added, his voice so easy, so normal, like he hadn't just turned my insides into knots.

I opened my mouth, but nothing came out. My heart was racing, my mind scrambling for anything to say. But all I could do was stand there, frozen, watching him as he waited for a response I couldn't seem to give.

He shifted slightly, his hands sliding into his pockets as his smile lingered. "It's really good to see you," he said, almost like he meant it.

My mouth felt dry. The cashier's voice broke through the haze, calling my name loudly from the counter.

I turned my head toward her, my body moving on autopilot. She was waving the bag of food at me, and I forced my legs to move. My hands shook as I grabbed the bag, clutching it tightly to my chest like a shield.

I didn't look back at him as I headed for the door. I couldn't. If I did, I might have said something I'd regret. Or worse, I'd say nothing and let him walk away thinking he'd won.

The sun greeted me as I stepped outside, but I barely felt it. All I could think about was the look on his face, the way he spoke, the way he seemed... fine. Better than fine.

Maybe Another Time

Was I... was I the problem?

I was left standing in the heat, holding a bag of takeout and wondering why it took him losing me to become the man I begged him to be.

CHAPTER 5: DOSAGE OF DESPAIR

The office felt quieter this morning, or maybe I was just tuning out the usual buzz. My hands automatically moved as I prepared Mrs. Grayson's treatment plan, double-checking the dosages and notes I'd meticulously compiled over the past few days.

I focused on her smile from our last conversation and the warmth in her eyes when she talked about finally feeling stronger.

I could still feel the weight of last night, the way Derek's face lingered in my mind long after I locked my door. My chest felt tight just thinking about it. It wasn't just that he seemed put together; it was how he carried it. This new version of him had always existed, and I just wasn't good enough to receive it.

The way he smiled was so normal. Like nothing had ever happened, or like I hadn't spent years begging him to get it together while he told me to be patient, to wait, to trust that he'd come through.

Now, he suddenly had a job, and he'd "handled" things with Charlene like it had always been that easy all along.

Was I the one holding him back? Was I too demanding, too impatient, too... too much? I didn't think I'd ever be the kind of person to ask myself that, but there it was, hovering in the quiet like it had been waiting for me to notice.

I thought I'd been guiltily hoping—no, expecting—that the next time I saw him, he'd be groveling, apologizing, and begging me to come back. That is the fantasy, right? The one where you walk away, and they fall apart without you?

But he didn't fall apart. He stood in that stupid polished outfit, saying things like "It's all good" and "I hope you're doing well" while I felt like my world was sinking.

The printer hummed behind me, snapping me back to reality as the last pages slid neatly into the tray. I grabbed the papers and clipped them together, smoothing out the edges like that would make the mess in my head any neater.

I told myself I'd drop this off at Mrs. Grayson's room and spend the rest of the day drowning in tasks. That's how I deal with most things: I work until there's no space left for spiraling thoughts or stupid memories of Derek's perfect haircut.

The printer beeped, a cheerful little sound that meant I was done here, but my fingers still clutched the counter as voices filtered in from down the hallway.

I glanced up as Tania rounded the corner, flanked by Kara and Dr. Patel. Her laugh was sharp enough to cut glass. Kara was carrying her iced coffee, the condensation dripping onto her scrubs, while Dr. Patel looked up from his tablet, frowning slightly like he was wondering why he bothered leaving his office.

I stiffened, trying to root myself in place, but the fight and flight response gripped my body. My fingers curled tighter against the counter as Tania stopped just outside the breakroom, gesturing wildly with one hand while clutching her phone in the other.

She was holding out her left hand, flashing something that caught the light.

The ring.

The printer beeped again, but the sound barely registered as my gaze locked onto her hand. She twisted her wrist, angling the ring to sparkle even brighter, drawing attention to it like she'd done this a hundred times already.

Kara gasps, clutching her iced coffee like it might slip out of her hand. "Oh my God, Tania! Is that—"

"Yup." Tania tossed her hair over her shoulder, her wide smile practically blinds. "I mean, I know it's sudden, but when you know, you know, right?"

The nurses around her erupted in a predictable chorus of gasps and coos, murmuring congratulations, but it all blurred into static for me.

I grabbed the papers from the tray, trying to retreat into myself, when I bumped into someone.

"Whoa there," Beattie said softly, steadying me with a hand on my elbow. I mumbled an apology, my voice barely audible over the noise of the breakroom. "Don't stay around for this, Imara... keep it moving."

She said nothing else; she squeezed my arm lightly before moving past me. I should have followed her; I wanted to.

"He proposed just a few days ago. It was so romantic! We went to La Fortuna—that little Italian spot downtown. Candlelight, wine, the works. And right in the middle of our dessert, he gets down on one knee."

"And this ring." Tania stretched her hand out even further, her smile so wide I could have sworn it was practically dripping off her face. "He picked it out himself. Perfect fit. He said he didn't even need to ask my size. He just... knew."

She said it like poetry, her voice softening as if reciting a love sonnet. "He just knew. My gaze flickered to her hand for the final time, and I felt like I Would snap.

I turned on my heel and walked away. I didn't look back. By the time I reached the end of the hall, I ducked into an empty supply closet, shutting the door behind me. I just stood there, gripping the fabric of my scrub pants.

The tears came, spilling over in hot, silent streams. I sunk to the floor, my legs trembling as I let myself fold into the small space. The papers I'd been clutching fell into my lap, forgotten.

Less than a month! It had been less than a month since I walked into that room and saw them together. His hands were on her, and her lips were on his. Less than a month after finding out he was sleeping with Tania, he was... engaged. Getting married. Planning a life with her, the life I thought was mine.

I shook my head, the bitterness rising in my throat. "He just knew," she said.

Of course, he did. Derek always knew how to make something sound perfect, like he'd rehearsed it in front of a mirror. And she's eating it up like it's the gospel truth.

The thought made me laugh, a short and bitter laugh, the sound catching in the quiet. It didn't help. It felt like the dam was cracking, and everything I'd been holding in for weeks was finally spilling out. Anger, hurt, and humiliation came rushing back, fresh and raw.

I didn't even realize I was sobbing until the sound of it echoed in the small closet. The raw, guttural noise feels foreign, like it's coming from someone else. I pressed my hands over my mouth, desperate to stifle it, but it was too late.

The sound of the door creaking open jolted me. I froze, wiping at my face with the sleeves of my scrubs, scrambling to pull myself together. Of course. Of course, someone would find me here like this.

"Imara?" Beattie's voice was soft, and when I glanced up, her kind eyes met mine. She didn't look surprised, just... understanding. She stepped in quietly and shut the door behind her without a word.

I expected her to say something—ask what was wrong, tell me it would be okay, and offer some good advice I couldn't handle in that moment. But she didn't. She just sank next to me on the floor.

Eventually, my breathing steadied, the sobs tapering off into small, shaky inhales. I risked a glance at her, and she gave me a faint smile—not pitying, just present like she was waiting for me to speak first if I wanted to.

"Beattie," I said, my voice hoarse, barely above a whisper. "Tell me more about the relocation program."

She raised an eyebrow, her lips curving into a small, knowing smile. "I was wondering when you'd ask." She leaned against the wall, drawing one knee up as she studied me. "There's a spot in Vermont. It's six months and includes decent pay, housing, and even help to move. At the end of the term, if you like it, you can stay on."

Vermont?

"Six months?"

Beattie nodded, her expression softening just a bit. "Yeah. It's a good deal. It's a quiet place with a slower pace than here. If you're looking for a change... I'd say go for it."

I nodded slowly, the ember of thought from before reigniting in my chest.

"Let me know if you're interested. I can pull the details for you."

Six months in Vermont.

"Okay," I said finally, the word leaving my lips before fully committing. "Yeah. Send me the details."

CHAPTER 6: SCARVES AND SINKHOLES

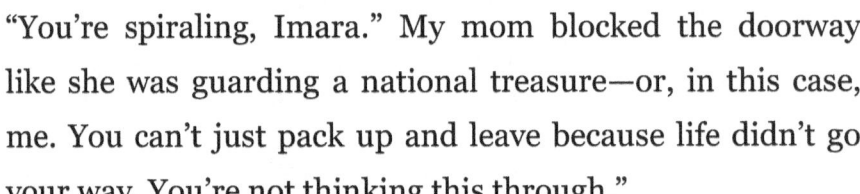

"You're spiraling, Imara." My mom blocked the doorway like she was guarding a national treasure—or, in this case, me. You can't just pack up and leave because life didn't go your way. You're not thinking this through."

I folded a sweater, shoving it into the already overflowing suitcase. "I am thinking," I shot back. "For the first time in months, I'm actually thinking about what I need. And what I need is to get out of this state."

Her arms crossed tighter, her stare pinning me in place. "And go where? To some snowy place you've never been? Alone? Imara, be serious. This is ridiculous."

"I'm twenty-six, Mama!" I snapped, spinning around to face her. "I'm a grown woman. I'm almost thirty, and yet I'm sitting here in my childhood bedroom, sleeping under the same Cheetah Girls poster I begged for in sixth grade. Do you know what that feels like? It feels like failure."

Her face shifted. For a moment, I regretted the words. But before I could soften them, she was stepping closer. "Failure? So that's what this is? After everything we've done for you, you think coming back here was failing?"

"Mama, that's not what I—"

"No," she trembled, "We took you in, Imara. When he—" She broke off, shaking her head like Derek's name was poison. "We were here for you. We helped you get back on your feet, and now you want to just... run away like none of that matters?"

"That's not what I meant!" I argued, my voice raising. "I needed you both then, and I'll always be grateful. But I can't keep doing this. Staying here, feeling stuck, it's... suffocating."

She exhaled sharply."Running away isn't healing," she said, softer now. "It's just running."

Before I could respond, my dad stepped into the room. His presence filled the space, calm and steady, like a deep breath I couldn't seem to take. "Marcia," he said gently, resting a hand on her shoulder.

She glared at him, but after a moment, she stepped back, her arms crossed so tightly that it was a wonder she was still breathing. My dad looked at me, his face softer but still serious.

"Six months, Imara..." he whistled, pursing his lips together. "Six months in someplace you don't know, where no one knows you? That's a long time to be alone. What happens when it gets hard and you need someone? We won't be there to help."

"That's the point, Daddy," I held out my hands. "I need to figure this out on my own. I can't keep leaning on you and Mom every time life punches me in the face."

He studied me for a long moment, his lips pressed in a thin line. "We just don't want you to feel like you're fighting this alone."

"And I love you both for that," I said, my throat tightening. "But I have to do this. I can't... I can't stay here. I'll lose my mind."

My mom let out a bitter laugh, muttering something under her breath that sounded suspiciously like, "She already has."

Without another word, she spun on her heel and walked out, her shoulders tense. The sound of her retreating footsteps felt like a door slamming in my chest.

My dad lingered, his hand resting on the doorframe. "She'll come around," he said quietly. "Just give her some time."

The cab jerked slightly as it turned down a quiet street, tires crunching over the packed snow. My eyes darted to the driver, who met my gaze in the rearview mirror with a raised eyebrow.

He looked completely unbothered, like he'd been driving these icy roads forever. Meanwhile, I was clutching my bag like it was a life raft.

I glanced out the window, taking in the rows of houses that looked like something out of a snow globe—postcard-perfect with snow-covered rooftops, icicles hanging from eaves, and smoke curling from chimneys.

The heater hummed faintly, but it barely kept the cold at bay. My breath fogged the window as I shifted in my seat, pulling my coat tighter around me. Back home, the winter felt like a polite nudge; here, it was a slap across the face.

The cab driver cleared his throat, his eyes flicking back to mine for a second. "First time in Vermont?" he asked, his voice breaking the silence.

"Is it that obvious?" I asked, my tone falling between self-deprecating and hopefulness that he didn't press for details.

He chuckled, low and gravelly. "City folks always have that look. Like they're wondering if they've made a mistake."

I forced a smile that said, "You're not wrong," but I was not about to admit it out loud. "Something like that," I muttered, glancing back out the window.

He cut the engine, and the sudden silence pressed in, leaving space for the nervous buzz in my head to grow louder. I stayed frozen, gripping the strap of my bag like it might hold me down if I tried to bolt. My feet didn't move. My brain didn't move.

I sat there for a bit longer than I should, staring at the modest duplex like it was a portal to another dimension, clutching my bag so tightly my fingers ached.

Out of the corner of my eye, I caught him tapping his finger against the steering wheel, the rhythmic tap-tap-tap growing louder in the silence. He shifted in his seat, awkwardly rocking back and forth like he was testing its durability, his lips rolling inward as if he was trying his best to bite back words.

Finally, he broke. "Here we are!" he said, his voice painfully cheery. His tone practically screamed, "Please leave."

"Right. Yeah. Thanks."

I fumbled with the door handle and stepped out into the icy air that seemed determined to remind me of all my life choices. The driver waited just long enough to see me make it to the snow-covered walkway before he drove off, leaving me standing there, my breath puffing out in frosty little clouds.

I glanced at the green shutters on the window of my unit, my stomach twisting. The duplex looked quaint, almost as if it was daring me to turn around and run. For a fleeting moment, my mind wandered back to the mess I left behind, and my dad's arms wrapped around me like he could will me to stay if he just held on tight enough.

I hoisted my bag over my shoulder and took my first step toward the porch. Except, my foot didn't lift—it stayed stuck, sucked into the snow.

My new home.

According to the listing, the apartment was small and modest. The walls were a soft cream, and the hardwood floors creaked slightly under my steps.

"Seriously?" I muttered, yanking my foot free with an unflattering squelch only to have the other sink just as deep.

My breath huffed out in annoyed clouds as I shuffled to the steps like a badly wrapped mummy.

When I reached the porch, my toes were soaked, my feet numb, and my mood was officially in the gutter. My coat, which I now realize was about as useful as a wet paper towel, clung to me in cold, soggy defeat. "Perfect. Love this for me," I said, slapping my gloves together to remove the snow. It didn't help. Nothing felt like it could help.

With a soft click, the key turned in the lock, and I shoved the door open, half expecting the universe to throw another curveball. But no, it opened without a hitch. Small mercies, I guess.

My new home.

The furnishings were basic but practical: a worn beige couch, a sturdy coffee table, and a small dining table with two mismatched chairs.

What pulled my attention, though, was the window. It was wide, framed by simple white curtains, and the view outside was straight out of a Lifetime movie: snow-dusted trees, tiny shops with glowing signs, and people bundled up in scarves as they shuffled by.

It was almost too perfect, as if the town was trying too hard to charm me.

I set my suitcase down in the corner and ran my fingers over the back of the couch. It was scratchy and stiff and would probably make my mom physically recoil. She'd call it "soulless" or something equally dramatic, followed by, "How do they expect you to feel at home when it looks like this?"

I shook my head, half-laughing at the thought, and made my way to the bedroom. It was just as plain as the living room: a bed with a mismatched quilt, a small dresser, and a mirror on the closet door. It was cozy, but only if I squinted.

The mirror caught my reflection, and I froze briefly, taking myself in. My hair, all flattened and staticky from the flight, was a total mess, and my face looked washed out except for the cold-induced flush on my cheeks. Tired. That's the best word for it. Tired in a way concealer couldn't fix.

I ran a hand through my hair, trying to calm it down. It didn't help much. I sighed and twisted a few strands back, pinning them out of my face before shrugging out of my sweater. Maybe I could shake this "I just crawled out of a carry-on bag" look if I tried a little harder.

The moment I took the sweater off, a sharp chill hit me, cutting straight through my long-sleeve shirt. "Nope, absolutely not," I muttered, pulling it back on so fast I nearly caught my hair in the fabric. Even inside, Vermont is freezing.

I glanced at the bed, hesitated for half a second, gave in, kicked off my boots—more like wrestling with them since they seemed intent on staying glued to my feet—and collapsed onto the mattress.

Everything about this moment felt like the end of something, but at the same time, the fragile, hesitant start of something else, something I didn't fully understand yet.

I closed my eyes, willing myself to get used to it, to make peace with the silence that came with living completely alone. Even on my previous travel nurse assignments, it was never this quiet—there were shared spaces, neighbors who were always just a knock away, and even the hum of the city outside the window.

I shifted slightly, letting out a long breath that felt too loud for the room. I'd have to get used to this: the quiet, the solitude, and the idea that this place is mine and mine alone. It was not the worst thing, not really. But it was unfamiliar, and that was what twisted in my stomach like an itch I couldn't scratch.

"Move it or lose it, Frosty."

I spun around, startled, just in time to barrel into a small, grumpy-looking woman clutching a cane. She stumbled back, glaring at me as if I'd personally offended her ancestors.

"Are you trying to kill me? Is that it? First day in town, and you're already plotting murder?" she barked, her voice cutting through the stillness like a car alarm.

My mouth opened, closed, and opened again. "What? Of course not, ma'am. I didn't see you there."

She huffed, adjusting her hat with a flourish. "Didn't see me? I'm practically glowing against all this snow! What are you, blind or just clueless?"

Before I could respond—apologize again or possibly defend myself—she waved a dismissive hand. "Bah, whatever. Just watch where you're going next time, city girl. Some of us don't have nine lives."

She started shuffling away, muttering under her breath about "out-of-towners with no sense," leaving me standing there as if I'd just failed some secret Vermont test. I adjusted one of my scarves, muttering to myself. "Great start, Imara. Just great."

I finally took in the hospital in front of me. The brick facade had snow dusting the edges like frosting on a cake. There were no bustling crowds or flashing ambulance lights. The place was just quiet, like it was holding its breath.

I tugged my scarf tighter, or rather, scarves. Three of them, to be exact. I probably looked like a slightly fashionable mummy, but I didn't mind it so much: being warm was all that mattered. Mostly. The cold still managed to sneak in, stinging my nose and cheeks.

My hand rested on the door handle briefly but long enough for the cold metal to seep through my glove. Then, with a quick pull, I was inside. Warmth washed over me instantly, the heater doing its best to erase the chill from outside.

The lobby was small but welcoming, with polished floors that gleamed under soft lighting. A few patients sat scattered across the waiting area, bundled in coats and flipping through magazines. There was a subtle hum of conversation, and nurses moved purposefully yet without the frantic energy I was used to. It was almost unsettling how calm everything felt.

A nurse behind the reception desk looked up and offered me a polite smile. "Can I help you?"

"Uh, yeah." I cleared my throat, pulling off my gloves as I approached. "Imara Hastings. I'm, uh, new. Starting today?"

Her smile widened, her eyes scanning a clipboard. "Oh, right. Welcome. You'll want to head up to the second floor. That's where orientation is; you can't miss the big red and yellow sign."

"Thank you." I stepped away, pulling my scarf loose as I headed toward the elevator. My boots squeaked faintly against the polished floors, their sound oddly amplified in the quiet.

A nurse passed me, her head buried in a clipboard, barely sparing me a glance. No one looked at me twice, no curious stares or hushed whispers about the "new girl." I like it.

The ride to the second floor was mercifully short. When the doors opened, a bold, almost cartoonish red and yellow sign that screamed "Orientation Room," including an unnecessary number of exclamations, greeted me.

I pushed open the door to reveal a room with neat rows of chairs and a projector humming softly in the corner. A handful of nurses were already here, scattered among the chairs in loose clusters. Most of them were deep in conversation, their voices low but animated. As I walked in,

I caught bits and pieces: something about someone's dog eating a pair of shoes, a recipe gone horribly wrong, and weekend plans involving snowmobiles.

The door opened again, and a tall woman walked in front of them with an air of presence that made everyone immediately straighten in their chairs. She had her short gray hair swept neatly to one side, and she was clutching a clipboard like it was a scepter. She didn't even have to say anything—she just looked like she ran this place.

She moved to the front of the room, set the clipboard on the table with a precise tap, and scanned the room. "Good morning, everyone. I'm Linda Fletcher, the nurse manager here at Greenmont Medical. Welcome to orientation."

She clasped her hands in front of her, her posture straight, no-nonsense. "First off, congratulations. Being here means you've joined one of the most dedicated teams in the region. At Greenmont, we pride ourselves on providing excellent and compassionate care. Our vision is to set the standard for patient-centered healthcare, and our mission is simple: every patient, every interaction, every time."

She leaned slightly against the table, softening her stance just enough. "You'll see me on the floor often—don't be shy. Find me if you have questions or concerns or even need a moment to vent. I might not always have the answer right away, but I'll make sure you get one."

Her tone shifted slightly, a hint of warmth breaking through. "This is a challenging job—it's supposed to be—but it's also one of the most rewarding things you'll ever do. We'll push you, you'll learn, and you'll grow. And we're here to make sure you succeed."

With that, she straightened, glancing at her clipboard before giving a small nod. "Let's get started."

I approached the table, clutching my orientation packet against my chest, and cleared my throat softly. "Excuse me, Ms. Fletcher?"

She looked up, her sharp gaze landing on me. For a split second, I wondered if I made a mistake, but then her expression softened—just a bit—and she raised an eyebrow.

"It's Linda," she said, setting the clipboard down. "And you are?"

"Imara Hastings," I said, offering a small smile. "I just transferred here under my hospital's relocation program."

Her head tilted slightly, and I could tell she was sizing me up by the way her eyes flicked over me—not unkindly, just assessing. After a beat, she nods.

"Whew, I know it's tough to get accepted into those programs; you must be pretty good," she said, folding her arms. "What brings you to Greenmont?"

"Thank you. I just... I needed a change of pace. Different challenges, new environment. Plus, I've heard good things about the team here."

Linda's lips twitched like she was fighting back a smile. "Flattery already? I like you, Hastings."

I chuckled softly, relieved by her tone. "Just being honest."

"Well, honesty will get you far here," she said, her voice firm but warm. "We don't sugarcoat things at Greenmont—

patients, staff, or otherwise. But we do work hard, and we support each other. You've got experience, which means I'll expect you to hit the ground running. Think you can handle that?"

I met her gaze, standing a little straighter. "Yes, ma'am. Absolutely."

"Good," she said, nodding approvingly. "You've got the look of someone who knows their way around a hospital. I'll see you out on the floor soon enough. If you need anything, don't hesitate to come find me."

"Thank you," I said, and I meant it.

CHAPTER 7: SMALL WINS

If there's one thing I learned on my first day at Greenmont, it's that the receptionist at the front desk—Hannah, I think—runs the place more than anyone else. She spent ten minutes explaining the coffee machine hierarchy, complete with a warning about the "espresso button of doom" that apparently short-circuited the entire breaker. I didn't even dare press for details.

The apartment always greeted me with the kind of silence that made every little sound louder: the hum of the fridge, the faint creak of the floorboards, and the relentless ticking of the clock that I swear had grown louder since I left this morning.

I set down the dish I had just washed, wiping my hands on a towel, before stepping back to survey the kitchen. A pot of pasta cooled on the stove, and a single, neatly portioned plate sat waiting on the counter.

My dinners had become simple affairs—just enough to keep me going. Tonight, it was spaghetti with store-bought marinara and a sprinkle of parmesan. It was not my mom's famous Sunday stew, but it would do.

I carried my plate to the tiny table by the window, sat, and stared at the darkened town square below. Across the road, an old man was using a shovel to clear his walkway—or at least trying to.

He attacked the snow as if it had personally insulted him, muttering under his breath as he tossed chunks of it to the side.

I laughed softly, shaking my head. "You tell that snow, sir," I murmured to myself. The sound of my voice broke the silence and startled me.

Yeesh.

For a second, I let myself think this moment was enough. I was here, in my own space, eating a meal I made myself, looking out at a peaceful little town. Accomplished, independent, and adulting like a pro.

But who was I kidding? It was lonely and sad.

I poked at the remaining spaghetti with my fork, swallowing the lump in my throat. For years, dinners were a shared event: it was usually either Derek cooking while I cleaned or me cooking while he told me what he'd do differently if he were in charge. Annoying as it was, at least it was noise.

After eating, I cleaned up quickly and wandered into the living room, sinking into the couch and pulling my phone from my pocket. The screen lit up, and my thumb hovered over the call icon as I scrolled through my contacts.

Mom. Dad. Even Jason and the rest of the guys. Their names stared back at me, but I couldn't bring myself to press call. I should give them time; they were probably still upset. I didn't want to hear the hurt in their voices, the unspoken question: Why couldn't you stay? Why couldn't you let us help?

Still, I had to accept my reality: I was hundreds of miles away, in a strange apartment with no one to talk to.

I thought about dialing anyway, just to hear their voices, but the thought of hearing the hurt—the disappointment—in them made my chest tighten. So, I didn't.

Instead, I sat with the fact that I was hundreds of miles away, in a strange apartment that didn't feel like mine, staring at a half-empty living room with no one to talk to.

The irony wasn't lost on me. I did this for a living. As a travel nurse, I moved from place to place, helping people adjust to their new realities, often while ignoring my own.

I set the phone down on the coffee table and leaned back, closing my eyes. The quiet wrapped around me like a heavy blanket, and for a moment, I let myself feel its ache.

Maybe that's the point. Maybe I needed to get used to this solitude. If I couldn't stand being alone with myself, how was I supposed to heal?

I sighed, reaching for the remote to turn on the TV. The noise filled the room, cutting through the silence. It would do for now.

The next day, I wrapped myself up as if I was heading to the Arctic: double sweaters and thick socks, but despite that, I still felt the bite of the chill as I stepped into Greenmont. It was honestly starting to feel like I would never be warm again.

I made my way through the halls, greeting people with smiles as I passed.

When I reached the nurse's station, Linda was already there, perched on a stool with a steaming mug of tea in her hands. She had her glasses perched on the tip of her nose, and her neatly styled bun softened her round, warm face. She was laughing with another nurse.

"Imara!" she called out as soon as she spotted me.

"Good morning," I said, setting my bag down on the counter.

"Morning, sweetheart." Linda sipped her tea, her eyes sparkling behind her glasses. "How'd you sleep? Settling into that apartment, okay?"

I opened my mouth, the excuse teetering on the edge, but the words stalled out, snagged by the kind of look Linda gave. "Still getting used to it," I admit. "The place is nice, but it's... quiet."

Linda hummed knowingly, her smile softening. "That's normal. Give it time. And if it stays too quiet, call me. I know all the best spots to grab a coffee or a bite around here." She winked, setting her mug down before sliding a file across the counter toward me.

"Now, let's get you started," she said, tapping the file with a manicured nail. "I'm assigning you to Mrs. Evelyn Carter today. Long-term care. She's a bit... particular, but also one of my favorites."

"Particular?" I asked, raising an eyebrow as I picked up the file.

Maybe Another Time

Linda chuckled. "She's a character. She likes things her way and won't hesitate to tell you when you're doing it wrong. But she's as sharp as a tack and has a heart of gold once you get past the exterior."

I nodded, flipping the file open for a quick glance. "Anything I should watch out for?"

"Just her charm," Linda said, grinning. "She's recovering, but she's as stubborn as they come. She might try to convince you she doesn't need half the care she's supposed to get; you know how they get. Just don't take her grumbles personally. If you need anything—anything—come find me, okay? My door's always open."

"Thanks, Linda. I really appreciate it."

"Of course, hun," she said while reaching out to squeeze my arm.

I nodded and flipped open the folder to scan through the notes. Eighty-two-year-old Mrs. Carter had a history of heart failure, diabetes, and arthritis. I tucked the file under my arm and made my way to her room.

When I pushed open the door, a petite woman with a head full of snow-white curls greeted me. She was sitting upright in bed, her back straight and her hands busy working a pair of knitting needles; the yarn in her lap was a bold, unapologetic pink.

The room itself was tidy, almost obsessively so. A vase of fresh flowers sat on the nightstand, their bright petals contrasting sharply with the neutral tones of the walls and bedding. The TV mounted on the wall played an old black-and-white movie at a low volume, the flickering images casting faint shadows across the room.

"You're new," she stated matter-of-factly.

"I am," I replied. "Imara Hastings, your new nurse."

The rhythmic click of the needles pulled at something in my chest, and I felt a sudden ache I wasn't ready for. Mrs. Grayson's face flashed in my mind: her laughter, the way she'd pat the bed to invite me closer, her stories that always seemed to end with a quiet but meaningful life lesson. I didn't even get to say goodbye to her.

The sadness lingered for a moment before Mrs. Carter snapped me back to reality with a sharp, "Well."

Her lips pressed into a thin line as she resumed knitting, the needles moving with renewed vigor. "I hope you're better than the last one. Didn't listen worth a lick, that girl. I told her no milk in my tea, and guess what she brought me?"

"Milk?" I guessed, suppressing a smile.

She narrowed her eyes. "Milk. And lukewarm, at that. Might as well have handed me dishwater."

I chuckled softly, setting the file down on the small table by her bed. "I'll do my best to keep your tea preferences in mind, Mrs. Carter."

"You'd better. I like someone who pays attention. Especially since I've had to set so many of you straight already," she muttered. She picked up her knitting again, her needles clicking in a steady rhythm.

"How long have you been a nurse, then? Or are you one of those fresh-faced ones who think a degree means you know everything?"

I sat on the edge of the visitor's chair, holding her gaze evenly. "A little over a year," I admitted. "But I don't think I know everything, especially everything about what my patients want."

She hummed. "Guess you're still figuring out how to keep people alive without scaring them to death."

A small smile tugged at my lips despite myself. "Something like that."

I quietly picked up the blood pressure cuff from the supply cart. "Do you mind telling me how you feel today?"

She shrugged, her fingers never stopping their work. "Oh, you know. Everything aches. That new medicine they put me on makes me feel like I've got ants crawling under my skin. And don't get me started on the food here. You'd think they were trying to finish us off."

I smiled faintly as I wrapped the cuff around her arm. "Noted. I'll check on your meds and see if there's anything they can adjust. About the food, though, I'm not sure there's anything I can do."

Her gaze softened just a little as I inflated the cuff. "You've got good bedside manners," she said grudgingly. "Reminds me of my granddaughter. She's a nurse, too, and she's down in Boston. Smart girl. Always said I'd make a terrible patient, though."

"Would she be wrong?" I asked lightly, raising an eyebrow as the cuff deflated.

Mrs. Carter snorted, a sound that was more amused than offended. Thankfully.

"Probably not."

By the time I stood to leave, Mrs. Carter was watching me with an almost approving look. "You're thorough," she said. "I'll give you that."

"Thorough is my specialty," I replied, tucking the chart under my arm. "And I'll remember: no milk in the tea." Her lips twitched, but she didn't smile outright.

"Add two sugars. Don't make me chase you down."

I grinned, holding back a laugh.

"Consider it done."

As I stepped into the hallway, I felt a little lighter. Tucking a difficult patient under my wing was a tiny victory, but it was enough, especially in a week plagued with doubt.

CHAPTER 8: MISMATCHED FAIRY LIGHTS

I had started waking up earlier and carving out quiet moments just for myself before the day took over. My mornings now began in the cozy little kitchen, wrapped in my fleece robe, cradling a steaming mug of tea as I tried to will myself into productivity.

I sipped my tea and glanced at the to-do list stuck to the fridge with a cheerful magnet shaped like a pine tree. Linda gave it to me on my first day, along with a warm smile. "We all need reminders sometimes, don't we?" It was absurdly cute, but somehow it fit her.

My morning checklist was simple: tea, breakfast (if I have time), and the ever-lengthy process of getting ready for work. I'd started putting a bit more effort into my looks lately—nothing major, just a little gel here, hairspray there, and some foundation—enough to feel like I was stepping into the day with a little more confidence.

Today, I chose a cozy knit sweater under my scrubs, gold studs in my ears, and a quick swipe of mascara. As practical as it was, it made me feel put together and like I was reclaiming some small piece of myself.

Once I was ready, I grabbed my bag, shrugged into my thickest coat, and braced myself for the walk to the car.

I still couldn't get used to Vermont winters, though. Even with the thermostat set perfectly, it was like the cold had a personality here: relentless and eager to sneak under every scarf and jacket.

The previous week, I'd spent twenty minutes figuring out how to scrape the ice off my windshield without scratching it. Yesterday, I'd wrestled with the key fob for five minutes before realizing I'd been pressing the wrong button the whole time.

Today, as I stepped outside, I was greeted by a snowdrift that had half-buried the front bumper.

"Of course," I muttered, clutching my bag tighter. I stopped, staring at the car like it had personally betrayed me. Then I bursted out laughing.

The sound, loud and unhinged, echoed through the quiet lot, and before I knew it, I had doubled over, clutching my sides. It was the kind of laugh that felt almost freeing, or like I'd finally lost it, but in the best way possible.

When I finally stopped, I straightened up, wiping my eyes with gloved hands. My breath puffed out in short, visible bursts as I cleared my throat and glanced around, suddenly self-conscious.

I scanned, making sure no one was peeking out their windows, before muttering to myself, "Well, that's one way to start the day."

I grabbed the snow brush from the back seat and set to work, brushing off the car with renewed determination. The cold seeped into my gloves, and my face stung from the wind, but I kept going.

By the time I pulled into the hospital parking lot, I couldn't help but feel a small sense of accomplishment. Vermont's cold might have it out for me, but I was learning to hold my own.

Once inside, I shrugged off my coat and headed toward the lounge for a quick coffee before starting my shift. As I poured myself a cup, I heard a voice that was somehow both melodic and bursting with energy.

"Oh my gosh, you must be Imara!"

I turned and found myself face-to-face with a woman who looked like she had walked straight out of a magazine for "bohemian chic." Her bright red hair was in a swept-up, loose bun, strands escaping artfully around her face. She was wearing a flowy cardigan with a mismatched pattern over her scrubs and clogs painted with tiny daisies.

"Hi," I said cautiously, unsure of how to handle this woman's whirlwind personality. "That's me."

"I'm Caroline!" she exclaimed, clasping her hands together. Her bracelets clinked merrily with the movement. "I've been out for two weeks, so I didn't get to welcome you the way I would've liked—a trip to this amazing yoga retreat—but I've heard all about you! Everyone says you're a natural."

Her enthusiasm caught me off guard and pulled a smile out of me before I could think better of it. "Nice to meet you, Caroline. I'm... glad you've already heard good things."

She tilted her head, her grin sharpening with a mischievous edge. She leaned forward slightly, resting her forearms on the counter like we were already co-conspirators. The faint clink of her name badge against the desk pulled my focus back to her eyes—bright and welcoming.

"Your energy is just... amazing. You know that? Yes, there's a bit of sadness, but it could be from the cold. Listen, we're having a staff dinner tonight; nothing fancy, just some of us letting loose. You're coming, right?"

"Oh, I don't know," I began, but she was already shaking her head.

"No excuses! You're new, and we don't bite. Well, if you challenge him to trivia, Sam might, but that's part of the fun." Her grin widened, and before I knew it, I was nodding.

"Sam?" I asked, furrowing my brow.

Caroline spun back around, her bracelets jingling as she clutched her coffee in her hand like it was a prized possession. "Dr. Whitaker! You haven't met him yet? He's, like, the hospital's golden man. Super smart and super nice, but don't let that fool you. He's ruthless when it comes to board games and random facts."

I raised an eyebrow, intrigued despite myself. "Good to know."

"You'll see what I mean tonight. Let's exchange numbers before you leave so I can text you the address!" She winked and pointed a finger at me before sauntering down the hall, humming a tune I didn't recognize.

I watched her go, still processing the whirlwind of Caroline, a trivia-loving doctor named Sam, and a staff dinner where I'd be the new face in the room.

That sounded like more than I had bargained for.

"You ready to brave the cold?" Caroline teased, leaning against the edge of the common room couch, her jacket half on as she watched me wrestle with my scarf.

She looked effortlessly warm in her patchwork coat, the colorful patterns clashing in the most charming way imaginable. Linda chuckled as she adjusted her sleek black gloves.

I grimaced playfully. "Born and raised in the South. This is... not my natural habitat. Is it possible to ever be ready?" I muttered, glancing at the frost-painted window as the wind outside howled like it had something to prove.

Caroline grinned, pulling her gloves out of her pocket and snapping them on with exaggerated flair. "Not really. But if we stay out there long enough, you'll be so frozen you won't feel it anymore."

Linda gave me a sympathetic smile. "Stop it, Caroline. Imara, you'll acclimate. Though I doubt you'll ever like it. We've lived here our entire lives, and we still struggle." She nodded toward the door, and I followed them out.

"Gah!" I hissed, yanking my coat tighter around me.

The wind slapped my face like it had a personal vendetta, and my short pixie cut was—I'm sorry—absolutely useless. I've had this style for years because it was easy, low maintenance, and made me feel like I had my life together. Sometimes. But on days like today, I'd trade every ounce of that practicality for the extra insulation of a messy bun or a head of thick braids.

Caroline laughed as she tugged a beanie over her smoothed-over red hair; gone was the bun. "Poor thing. You're gonna freeze before we even make it to the car."

"I just might," I muttered, half-joking, as I hustled after them.

The chill only worsened as we stepped outside. Snow crunched under my boots as I followed Caroline into the parking lot.

We piled into our cars, my hands practically glued to the heater vents as I waited for the windshield to defrost. Caroline's taillights flickered ahead, and I chose to follow her instead of fumbling with the directions she'd sent earlier. When we pulled up to her house, I realized I wouldn't have missed it anyhow because it was a complete reflection of her personality.

A string of mismatched fairy lights lined the porch. Potted plants clustered near the door, some looking a bit miserable in the winter air, while a wind chime made of seashells tinkled faintly in the breeze.

Caroline hopped out of her car, her breath puffing into the cold air as she waved me over with a wide grin. "Welcome to Casa Caroline," she called, her voice bright against the winter gloom. "Mismatched fairy lights, half-dead plants, and all. It's basically Martha Stewart meets... well, not Martha Stewart."

I laughed, stepping carefully over a patch of ice as I carefully made my way toward her. Inside, the warmth hit me instantly, and I took a moment to soak it in as I kicked off my boots by the door.

The living room was full of colorful tapestries, an assortment of plants on every windowsill, and shelves lined with crystals, books, and what looked like a collection of tiny, hand-painted teacups. A large dreamcatcher hung near the window, and the faint scent of sage lingered in the air.

"Beautiful, isn't it?" Linda said, hanging her coat on a wooden rack shaped like tree branches. "I wouldn't do the same to mine, but it always makes me smile to come here and see her personality sprawled everywhere. It's one of a kind."

"Thanks!" Caroline called from the kitchen, her voice carrying over the hum of conversation as she arranged a spread of catered food on the counter. "And by one of a kind, she means cluttered but cozy. Emphasis on the cluttered."

I grinned, following Linda toward the kitchen. "Did you make all this?" I asked, gesturing to the trays of food.

Caroline snorted, tossing a pair of tongs onto the counter. "Please. Do I look like I had time to whip up chicken parm and roasted veggies after a twelve-hour shift? I ordered it earlier. Marty from the deli down the street dropped it off. I told him to make it look homemade, and voilà!" She gestured dramatically to the spread.

Caroline beamed as she poured steaming water into a teapot shaped like a cat. "Tea while we wait? Everyone's always fashionably late to these things."

Caroline handed me a steaming mug of tea that smelled like it belonged in a spa: herbal, with a soft hint of mint and chamomile. As I wrapped my hands around it, the warmth seeped through the ceramic and into my fingers, and I let the scent rise to my nose before taking a small sip.

The front door creaked open every so often as more people trickled in, bringing with them bursts of cold air and snippets of conversation. As they shrugged off their jackets, laughter bubbled up in small pockets, and the room started to hum with a quiet kind of chaos.

I leaned against the counter, fingers lightly tracing the rim of my mug, letting the noise wash over me. The kitchen smelled like garlic bread and roasted veggies, the kind of scents that could convince anyone to relax.

I caught a glimpse of myself in a small, oval mirror hanging on the wall. My reflection felt like a stranger's: short, dark hair styled neatly, soft brown eyes that still looked a little tired, and skin that glowed faintly under the warm light. I slightly straightened my shoulders and reminded myself that I belonged here, even if I didn't quite feel it yet.

Caroline nudged me gently with her elbow, breaking my thoughts. "You good?"

I nodded, a small smile playing on my lips. "Yeah. I'm good."

By the time Caroline swung open the door again, the room was alive with chatter. Another gust of icy wind swept in, carrying along the sound of boots crunching on the porch. A tall figure stepped inside, shaking off the cold like it was a second coat.

He paused, eyes scanning the room, and for a moment, the energy shifted.

"Sam, close the door before we all turn into popsicles!" Caroline called out.

The broad-shouldered man with hazel eyes gave her a lopsided grin.

"You know I like to make an entrance," he said smoothly, pulling a small paper bag from under his arm. "Here's your monthly woo-woo delivery."

Caroline narrowed her eyes at him. "If that's another batch of your homemade elderberry syrup, you can keep it."

He handed her the bag, and she hesitantly took it, closing one eye as she peered in. Caroline gasped dramatically as she pulled out two crystals. "Ooooh, rose quartz! My aura thanks you, Dr. Whitaker."

"Rose quartz?" he teased, shrugging off his coat to reveal a navy sweater that clung to his frame like a high-end fashion designer had custom-tailored it to fit him and only him. "Amateur hippie. You can thank me when your energy's fully healed."

"Don't push your luck," Caroline quipped, tucking the crystals into her pocket.

"Stop being one," he fired back easily before turning his attention to the room again. He scanned the faces casually—until his gaze landed on me.

He froze.

It was subtle, just a slight hesitation, but it was enough to make my stomach twist. His eyes widened slightly like he wasn't expecting to see. I shifted awkwardly under his gaze, suddenly hyperaware of how my hair curls stuck up at certain points.

After a second, which felt like an eternity, his lips twitched into a smile. "I wasn't aware we were upgrading Caroline's lame dinners to include models."

Caroline smacked his arm. "Don't you dare call my dinner lame again, Sam. And leave Imara alone."

"Imara," he repeated, drawing the syllables out slightly. His smile softened, and he stepped forward, extending a hand. "Dr. Sam Whitaker. I don't believe we've met."

"Hi," I said, my voice coming out quieter than I would have liked as I shook his hand. "Imara Hastings. I just started at the hospital last week."

He raised an eyebrow and released my hand but kept his gaze on me. "A newbie? Well, welcome to the Green Mountain State. Caroline's dinner parties are your real initiation. Totally not boring or anything."

"Behave," Caroline warned.

Sam chuckled. "Fine, fine. I take it back," he said, throwing up his hands in mock surrender. He glanced back at me, his grin playful. "This party is... adequate. But with you here? It feels like maybe we've upgraded to 'borderline interesting.'"

I felt my cheeks warm up as I let out a small laugh, and in that moment, I caught it: the faint, woodsy scent clinging to him. It was something warm, like cedar, and a hint of spice.

Without missing a beat, Sam pulled out the chair directly across from me and sank into it with ease, resting an elbow on the table. The chatter in the room continued around us. It felt like we'd entered a personal bubble at that moment.

"Tell me, Imara," he said as he leaned forward slightly, his hazel eyes studying me with a curiosity that felt disarming. "How's your first week been? Are you surviving, or should we call it quits and get you back to someplace warmer?"

The corners of my mouth tugged upward despite myself. "Surviving. Mostly."

"Good to hear," he said, nodding. "Stick with us long enough, and you'll forget what warmth feels like anyway."

Linda rolled her eyes from across the table, a glass of cider in her hands. "Don't scare her off, Sam. We just got her."

"I'm not scaring," he replied, holding up his hands again. "I'm being honest. That's what good neighbors do."

"And curiosity," he added smoothly, leaning in just a fraction. His tone softened, but there was a weight to his next words. "Any elaborate story about how you got to relocate? Or why even?"

The question hit me like a slow-building wave. My fingers tightened around the mug as my pulse quickened, a faint warmth creeping up the back of my neck. I could feel the weight of his steady and searching gaze, but what made it worse was the subtle hush that had fallen over the room.

I glanced around quickly, confirming what I already felt: Caroline's half-turned toward me, clearly listening, and a few others were definitely in on the act, even if they were pretending not to be.

I swallowed hard, the words catching in my throat as I tucked a nonexistent strand of hair behind my ear. "Oh, it's not much of a story," I started, but my voice wavered just enough to betray me.

Caroline pounced immediately, leaning on the table with an exaggerated sigh. "Please. We've all been pretending not to eavesdrop for five minutes now, but let's be real: we're dying to know."

Her bluntness drew a ripple of laughter from the group, but all it managed to do was make my chest feel tighter. I set the mug down, my hand brushing over the edge of the table as if smoothing invisible crumbs. "Really, it's nothing exciting," I tried again, my voice quieter this time.

Caroline shot me an incredulous look. "You packed up your life and moved to the land of eternal frostbite. That alone is fascinating. Was it for love? Revenge? Witness protection?"

"Caroline," Sam said, his tone easy but laced with just enough firmness to make her pause. "Let her answer."

I glanced at him, and his hazel eyes were locked on mine, not probing, not teasing, but calm and steady, like he was trying to reassure me that I was in control of what I said next.

The words stuck in my throat anyway. My fingers fidgeted with the edge of my sleeve, my nails catching the fabric.

"Well, I've been a nurse for a little over a year now," I hesitated, not wanting to say too much. "I worked at a hospital there for a bit as a traveling nurse before deciding to, um, branch out. A fresh start, sort of."

Caroline leaned back slightly, her expression shifting to something softer, though her curiosity was still written all over her face. "A fresh start, huh?" she said, less dramatic this time. "Okay, I'll take it. For now."

The group's attention slightly shifted as someone made a joke, and the noise level in the room rose again.

Sam, though, didn't move. "Fresh starts are underrated," he said low enough that it felt like it was meant just for me.

Are we talking about the same Mrs. Carter who would hiss at people if she could?" He pressed a hand to his chest as if someone had just told him that pigs were flying.

The room erupted into laughter, and I found myself laughing, too, the sound loosening something tight in my chest. Everyone seemed to know exactly what he was talking about; their knowing chuckles were a shared inside joke.

"She's not that bad," I said, though my grin gave me away.

"Not that bad?" Sam echoed, raising an eyebrow. "This is the same Mrs. Carter who threw a tissue box at me last year for suggesting she switch to decaf."

The laughter grew louder, and Caroline clapped her hands together. "Oh, I forgot about that! Didn't she call you a 'soulless bean-hater' or something?"

"Close," Sam said, grinning. "It was 'bean-hating quack.' Get it right."

I laughed again, shaking my head as I sipped my tea, the room's warmth settling around me. For the first time, I felt like I was not just a guest here. I felt part of something.

"So, Imara. You're smart, have a great sense of humor, a gorgeous smile... I don't want to go on, or else Cupid over there will sit with her cards tonight and twist our fate." Caroline all but launched a bone at him. "There must be someone special you left behind."

My smile faltered. It was slight, barely noticeable, but it was enough to make my stomach twist. For a split second, I considered brushing it off entirely, tossing out a joke, or deflecting with a laugh.

But, something in their warmth felt disarming. It felt like they were genuinely interested and not prying, as if they'd accept whatever I chose to share without judgment.

"Nothing worth mentioning, guys. I'm as single as can be... no special someone back home," I said lightly, keeping my tone breezy as I hoped the conversation would move on to something else.

Sensing the shift in moods, Linda chimed in. "If we're talking special, I had this patient who refused to take her medication unless I sang to her. Every. Single. Time. And not just any song—she had specific requests. Broadway numbers, Elvis, and even nursery rhymes. My rendition of 'Hound Dog' was so bad, I could swear that I almost got fired."

I caught Sam watching me out of the corner of my eye, his curiosity clearly not satiated.

"Do not let her fool you," Caroline cut in, grinning. "I've heard Linda sing, and it's not bad at all. She's just embarrassed that she secretly loved it."

Linda swatted her playfully, but the whole group laughed again.

The evening wound down, and I stood and mumbled something about needing to grab my jacket, nodding toward the foyer. Caroline waved me off with a grin.

"Don't let the cold knock you out! We need you alive for the next dinner."

As I tugged my thin coat off the rack, I braced myself to face the elements. The thought of stepping into the freezing Vermont night made me hesitate at the door, and I let out a small, involuntary groan.

"Not a fan of the cold, huh?" I turned to see Sam leaning against the wall, his hands tucked into his pockets, watching me with a knowing smirk.

"It's not my favorite," I admitted, pulling my coat on and wincing as the fabric barely covered my arms.

He raised a brow, then shrugged off his own jacket. It was big and dark, clearly made for someone a lot taller than me, and it looked like the coziest thing I'd ever seen.

"Here," he said, holding it out.

I blinked at him, surprised. "Oh, no. That's okay. I'm not stealing your jacket."

"You're not stealing it," he countered smoothly. "You're borrowing it. Big difference."

"I'll be fine," I insisted, even as I shivered just thinking about stepping outside.

Sam just chuckled and draped the jacket over my shoulders before I could protest further. The weight of it was immediate, heavy, and comforting, and it smelled faintly of cedar and something else I couldn't place. My protest died in my throat as the warmth wrapped around me.

"If it makes you feel better," he said with a teasing lilt, "I'll be at the hospital tomorrow. If it bothers you that much, you can drop it off at my office."

I looked up at him, caught off guard by how effortlessly charming he was. "You'll be at the hospital?" I asked, tugging the edges of the jacket closer.

He nodded, a small smile playing on his lips. "Yep. I float between hospitals in the state. Tomorrow's my day at yours. So, no excuses for freezing out there, alright?"

I huffed a laugh, shaking my head as I gripped the jacket tighter. "Fine. But only because I don't want frostbite."

"Fair trade," he replied, his grin widening.

For a moment, we just stood there, and I felt his gaze linger on me, but not in an intrusive way; in a quiet, curious way that made my chest feel a little tighter. I cleared my throat, stepping toward the door.

"Thanks," I murmured, suddenly unsure where to look.

"Anytime," he said easily, stepping aside as I pushed the door open.

The cold air rushed in, but with his jacket wrapped around me, it didn't sting as much. As I stepped out into the night, I glanced back to find him still standing in the doorway, his hands now tucked back into his pockets. He gave me a quick nod, and I returned it before heading to my car.

The drive home was quiet, the warmth of his jacket lingering long after I'd turned up the heater. For the first time in a long time, I found myself smiling—not for anyone else, but just for me.

CHAPTER 9: MEET-CUTE

The next morning, I found myself standing outside Dr. Whitaker's office, his jacket folded neatly in my hands. I hesitated momentarily and wondered if I should've just left it at the nurse's station. But then I thought about his easy smile and how he'd so casually loaned it to me last night without a second thought. It wouldn't hurt to thank him in person.

I knocked lightly, and his voice called out, "Come in."

I pushed the door open, and an entirely different side of Sam Whitaker greeted me. He was in full uniform—scrubs and a crisp white coat—and for a second, I faltered. Gone was the relaxed, playful guy from last night, replaced by someone who looked every bit the competent, professional doctor.

His hair was neatly combed, and there was a pair of reading glasses perched on his nose as he scanned a chart.

He glanced up, and a smile instantly lit his face, softening the polished exterior.

"Ah, if it isn't Vermont's newest model nurse."

I rolled my eyes but couldn't stop the small grin that crept onto my face. "You really need to retire that joke. I'm just here to return this." I held out the jacket.

He leaned back in his chair, his hands folding casually behind his head. "You could've kept it, you know. It looked better on you than it ever did on me."

"A deal's a deal, Dr. Whitaker. I borrowed it; now I'm returning it." I set the jacket on the edge of his desk, trying to ignore the flutter in my chest at his playful tone. "Thanks again."

"Anytime," he said smoothly, but then he frowned slightly. "Wait, have you had your coffee yet?"

I blinked at him. "Uh, no. I was planning to grab some after this."

He got up, moving toward the coffee machine in the corner of his office. "Perfect timing. Let me get you—" He paused, peering into the empty pot with a dramatic sigh. "And, of course, we're out."

"That's fine, really—"

"Sam," he corrected smoothly, his voice firm but warm. He stepped closer, the mug still extended, his gaze steady. "And it's not up for debate."

I hesitated, my fingers brushing over the edge of my scarf as I glanced at the steaming mug. It's tempting, but—

"You're freezing," he added, but with a hint of concern that made me glance up. His eyes flickered to my sweater, and he quirked an eyebrow. "I can only imagine how cold your organs must feel in that thin thing."

My eyes darted down to the sweater, and my cheeks flushed. Was it really that obvious? I tugged the hem awkwardly as if that would magically make it look warmer.

"It's not that bad," I muttered, but my attempt at brushing it off fell flat when my fingers betrayed me with a tremble.

Sam just smiled, tilting the mug toward me again. "Humor me," he said. "I'd feel better knowing you've got something warm, even if you insist you're fine."

I reluctantly reached for the mug, the heat seeping into my fingers the second I wrapped my hands around it. The warmth was immediate, spreading through my palms, and I had to hold in my groan.

"Thanks," I mumbled, taking the warm mug from his hands.

"See? Chivalry isn't dead," he said with a wink, sitting back down. "Though I'll admit, my motives are purely selfish. It's the least I can do for the person keeping my patients alive."

I shook my head, laughing softly. "I think you might be overestimating my role here."

"I doubt it," he said easily, leaning back in his chair.

I offered him a small smile and stood up, eager to put some distance between us.

"Thanks for the coffee, Dr.—Sam," I corrected myself quickly, and his smile deepened.

"Anytime, Imara."

For the first time in weeks, I didn't feel like I was dragging myself through the mud. It was not a big change, and it didn't mean much. But there was space now, however small, for a laugh or two between rounds. There was space for moments where I didn't feel like I was just surviving.

And if part of that was thanks to someone handing over a mug of coffee and reminding me that not everyone in the world is difficult? Well, I'd take it. Friends like that were hard to come by.

While turning the corner into my neighborhood, I caught sight of something new: a group of kids bundled up in mismatched scarves and coats so puffy they looked like tiny marshmallows, dragging sleds up the small hill near the park.

I slowed the car instinctively, watching as one of the kids launched down the slope, their sled kicking up a spray of powder. The squeal that followed was so loud and full of delight that it echoed all the way to the bottom, where they tumbled off in a heap of laughter. It was unfiltered, raw joy—the kind that could make anyone forget that anything else existed for a moment.

A small smile crept onto my face.

"Will I ever have this? I thought to myself.

Would I ever get to watch my own child, bundled in too many layers, their scarf half-dangling as they raced down a hill? Would I hear that kind of laughter and know it was mine?

I gripped the steering wheel tighter, the warmth from the heater suddenly doing nothing for the cold settling in my chest.

Would it even be here? With its frosty mornings and endless charm, would Vermont be the backdrop for a life I never got to build?

My fingers flexed as if they could shake the memory loose—the stark, sterile hospital room, the look on the doctor's face... crap.

I blinked hard, my vision blurring for a second before I shoved the thought back where it belonged, burying it deep beneath the noise of the kids' laughter.

When I glanced back at the slope, the kids were still at it, sledding, shouting, and piling snow onto one another. The world kept moving, even when mine felt like it had come to a standstill.

I pulled my eyes away and turned onto my street, the smile gone now.

"It's funny how a single moment of joy—someone else's joy—can dig up everything you've been trying so hard to forget," I thought.

I sighed, and just as I parked, I noticed movement across the way. Mrs. Harlow, the older woman who lived across from me, was perched on her porch swing. The swing creaked softly as she rocked back and forth, a thermos of tea cradled in her gloved hands.

When our eyes met, her face lit up in a smile, and she raised her thermos in greeting. "Evening, dear!" she hollered, her voice carrying over the icy wind.

I waved back, my fingers stiff from the cold, but she surprised me just as I was about to head inside. Setting the thermos down on the porch beside her, she pulled out what looked like a harmonica—no, it was a harmonica.

Before I could fully process what was happening, she lifted it to her lips and started playing.

The tune floated through the air like a marching band in a blender. My eyebrows quickly furrowed together. It was loud and completely off-key, each note warbling wildly as though the harmonica itself was struggling to stay on track.

I bit the inside of my cheek, trying not to laugh. My lips twitched as she kept going, absolutely unfazed by how truly awful it sounded. Somehow, the sheer confidence in her performance made it even better.

The heaviness that had weighed on me just moments ago— the thoughts I'd been trying to shove down—lifted so suddenly it was almost startling. I couldn't help the soft laugh that escaped my lips, but it grew until I clutched my coat like it would stop me from doubling over.

"Mrs. Harlow," I gasped between bursts of laughter, my breath visible in the cold air, "you're going to wake the entire neighborhood!"

Mrs. Harlow paused just long enough to shoot me a wink before diving back into her chaotic serenade, now even louder. It was so ridiculous, so wonderfully absurd, that the cold didn't feel quite as biting anymore.

"Best porch performer this side of Vermont!" she declared, loud enough for anyone nearby to hear.

I smiled, amusement tugging at the corners of my mouth and a flicker of secondhand embarrassment curling in my chest. I shook my head slightly, my breath puffing in the cold air, and wrapped my arms tighter around myself. "I'll take your word for it!" I called back, shivering as I stepped toward my apartment.

Mrs. Harlow grinned wide, clearly pleased with herself, as she picked up her thermos again. She took a slow sip, then paused, like a thought had just hit her. "Next time, bring requests!" she shouted.

I laughed under my breath, my shoulders shaking, but then she added, "Oh, and have you been to that little café on Main Street yet? Cozy place with great pastries. The new owner's a bit of a charmer."

That made me pause mid-step. I glanced over my shoulder, one eyebrow quirking up. "Not yet," I said, the words drawn out with cautious curiosity.

She perked up even more, her eyes twinkling in the porch light as if she'd been waiting for this moment. "Well, you should," she said, her tone suddenly conspiratorial. "He's quite the looker, too, if you're into the tall, dark, and handsome type." She winked dramatically. She was clearly casting me in some Hallmark movie.

I snorted, shaking my head again as I started to turn back toward my door. "I'll make sure to schedule a meet-cute."

"You do that, dear!" she called after me.

As I fumbled with my keys and glanced back, I caught her waving the harmonica in one hand and her thermos in the other, looking entirely pleased with herself.

CHAPTER 10:
COMPARTMENTALIZED

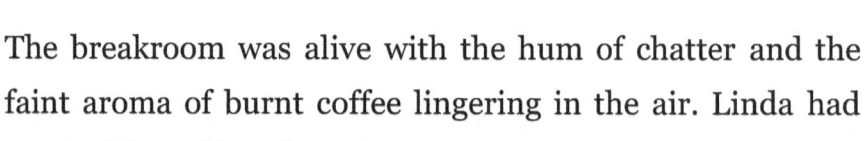

The breakroom was alive with the hum of chatter and the faint aroma of burnt coffee lingering in the air. Linda had perched herself on the edge of the counter, holding her mug like it was the only thing tethering her to sanity, while Caroline paced dramatically near the fridge.

"I'm telling you," Caroline groaned, her hands flying up in frustration. "This patient is out to ruin me. My aura? Destroyed. My chakras? All over the place. And don't even get me started on the energy in that room: it's cursed."

Linda snorted, shaking her head. "Or maybe it's because you called her 'sweetheart,' Caroline. She's 102 and cranky. She's probably seen more than a few things, and I doubt she enjoys placation."

Caroline looked up from her clipboard, her brow furrowing. "Placated? I wasn't placating her! I was being nice."

Linda raised an eyebrow, her expression both amused and skeptical. "Sure, but you've got to remember, someone who's made it past a century probably doesn't appreciate being called 'sweetheart.' She's lived through two world wars, survived the Depression, and seen more nonsense than we can imagine. I bet she heard 'sweetheart' and thought, 'Oh great, another young thing thinking I'm cute and helpless.'"

Caroline groaned, slapping the clipboard against her thigh. "I wasn't patronizing her! I call everyone sweetheart."

"Yeah, well, not everyone's Mrs. Sullivan," Linda replied, smirking. "You want to win her over? Drop the nicknames. Stick to 'Mrs. Sullivan' and ask her about something she knows you don't—like, oh, I don't know, the secrets of eternal life."

Caroline rolled her eyes but couldn't help grinning. "Fine. No more 'sweetheart.' But if she throws something at me again, I'm calling you to deal with it."

Linda raised her coffee cup in a mock toast. "Deal. But only because I want to see how she handles being called 'ma'am.'"

Caroline snorted, and I couldn't help but laugh along with them, imagining the fiery Mrs. Sullivan giving Caroline her signature death glare at the mere mention of another nickname.

"You'll survive, Caroline. I'm sure your chakras will bounce back."

Caroline groaned, muttering something about bad karma, and Linda patted her shoulder sympathetically. The sound of footsteps approaching the door caught my attention, and I glanced up to see Dr. Whitaker standing in the doorway.

"Imara," he said, gesturing toward the hallway. Would you mind if I stole you for a minute?"

Caroline wiggled her eyebrows at me, but I rolled my eyes and stood, smoothing down my scrubs. "Sure. What's up?"

"In my office, please."

I nodded, forcing a neutral expression, but my stomach tightened as I followed him down the hallway.

Did I miss something?

Forget to sign off on a chart?

My mind started a marathon spin of thoughts, trying to backtrack through everything I'd done that day.

I followed him down the corridor to his office. As the door clicked shut behind us, the shift in atmosphere was immediate. Papers and a half-empty coffee cup cluttered his desk, but he leaned against the edge.

"Is everything okay?" My brain was hard at work racing through every possible reason he could've called me in here, but his face didn't give me a single clue.

"Oh yeah, yeah. I just wanted to run something by you... I thought it would be better in private so I can explain better."

"Alright," I hummed, crossing my arms over my chest. "Shoot."

"We've got a community outreach program that serves some of the underserved areas nearby: health checks, basic care, that sort of thing. I think you'd be a great fit to join us."

"Wow... Sam, that sounds— I've never been part of something like that before," I admitted, shifting slightly on my feet. "It sounds important—really important. I just... I'm not sure I can give it my all right now. I'm still settling in, finding my footing here, and I'd hate to overcommit and end up letting anyone down."

That's exactly why I think you'd be a great fit. You don't do things halfway, Imara. You care, you think things through, and that's rare."

I hesitated, fiddling with the hem of my sleeve. "I-"

"Of course— no pressure. I know you've got plenty on your plate already. Just... think about it. I think you'd bring something special to the team."

"Thank you. I'll let you know."

"Good," Sam said, flashing a quick smile. He stepped back toward his desk and leaned against the edge again, crossing his arms in that relaxed yet authoritative way that somehow managed to feel both approachable and intimidating. "Oh, by the way—I was looking at Mrs. Carter's file earlier."

"You were?"

"Yeah," he said, nodding. "She's an interesting case, isn't she? A lot going on there. I noticed you've been working on adjusting her medication schedule and setting up a daily routine for her."

I nodded. "It seemed like the best way to get her compliance up. She's... particular about her timing, and I thought a structured approach might help."

"It's a good strategy. Just one thought, though. With her history of compliance issues, you might want to ease into the routine a bit slower. Maybe start with one adjustment at a time instead of a full schedule overhaul. Sometimes, patients like her push back harder if they feel overwhelmed. Just saying."

My smile faltered for a fraction of a second before I managed to steady it. "That's a good point. I'll keep that in mind."

Sam nodded. "She's lucky to have you, though. Not everyone would be willing to put in the effort it takes to figure her out the way you have."

"Thanks," I said, my tone a bit tighter than intended. Eager to excuse myself before my thoughts got the better of me, I glanced at the door and said, "I should get back to my rounds." I nodded, offered a polite smile, and then slipped out of his office.

As I walked down the corridor, my mind was buzzing. Part of me knew he meant well; he was probably used to mentoring newer staff and sharing his insights. But something about how he'd brought it up, so casually assuming I hadn't considered all the angles, rubbed me the wrong way.

It's not a big deal, I told myself firmly. He's kind, charming, and just trying to help. There's no need to read too much into it.

For now, I tucked it away, adding it to the growing pile of things I'd think about later—when I was not on the clock and not trying to navigate a hundred other things all at once.

CHAPTER 11: STITCHES IN TIME

When I opened the door to Ms. Carter's room and saw her sitting up in bed, her knitting needles moving steadily in her hands, a small flicker of relief warmed me.

"Well, if it isn't my favorite bossy nurse," she said without looking up.

I set her chart on the table and stepped closer. "Bossy? I thought I was just thorough."

She gave a skeptical hum but didn't argue. "Two things can be true at the same time, you know, Ms. Hastings. What are we doing today, then? More of your brilliant plans to 'improve my quality of life,' as you call it?"

"Actually, yes," I said, the corners of my mouth tugging upward despite myself. "But today, we're keeping it simple. Just one small change at a time. I thought we'd start with adjusting your afternoon medication to a little later. It might help with the drowsiness you've been feeling after lunch."

Her hands stilled, the yarn slipping between her fingers as she raised a sharp eyebrow at me. "You're serious?" she asked, her tone caught somewhere between surprise and cautious approval. "You actually listened to what I said?"

"Of course I listened," I replied, leaning forward slightly. "You said the early dose was messing with your afternoons. I figured we'd try something new."

She narrowed her eyes at me, the hint of a smile tugging at her lips. "Hmph. Well, maybe you're not just here to boss me around after all. But don't get too smug, Nurse Hastings. I'm still watching you."

I laughed softly, shaking my head. "I'd expect nothing less."

After a moment, she said, "You know," her voice softer, "most people don't bother asking. They just assume they know better."

"I don't know everything," I admitted, shrugging slightly. "But I'm getting to know you. And I figure you probably have a few good ideas of your own."

Her smirk returned, and she tilted her head, her gaze appraising. "You're all right, Hastings. For now."

"I'll take it," I replied, grinning as I made a note on her chart. Moments like these—her wit, her honesty—make it all worth it. "Anything else you need before I go?"

She waved a hand dismissively. "No, no. But don't forget my tea later. Two sugars, no milk."

I grinned as I stepped toward the door. "I wouldn't dream of it."

As I left her room, I felt a sense of satisfaction I hadn't felt in a while. I headed toward the nurse's station, the chart tucked under my arm. Halfway there, my phone vibrated in my pocket. I pulled it out, already expecting a reminder about some meeting or a group text from Caroline about bad hospital coffee.

Hey, heard you left the state for good? Call me when you can.

Derek.

My feet slowed, the words staring back at me like they were testing for a reaction. For a moment, there was one—a faint skip in my chest—call it muscle memory. But it fizzled just as quickly, leaving something close to indifference in its place.

I blinked at the screen, half-expecting something else to follow. An apology. A reason. A shred of effort.

"Call me when you can," I repeated to myself with a snort, shaking my head. "Yeah, I'll get right on that. Right after I've solved world hunger and invented time travel."

I slipped the phone back into my pocket without replying, shaking my head as I moved toward the station.

I found Linda leaning against the counter, her arms crossed over a few documents. Her bun was slightly loose, with a few strands escaping and curling around her face.

"Hey, you busy?" I said softly as I approached. "Got an update on Carter."

Linda glanced up, her eyes squinting slightly as though it took effort to focus. She gave me a quick, tired smile. "Let's hear it."

I set the chart on the counter and walked her through the medication adjustment and how Ms. Carter's grandson noticed she seemed more vibrant. Linda nodded along, her smile warming slightly, but there was something off: a tightness in her expression and a sheen of sweat on her forehead despite the chilly air.

"Linda, okay. Something's clearly off. What's wrong?"

She hesitated, pressing her lips together. Her cheeks were flushed, though I couldn't tell if it was from the heat of the station or something else entirely. "Yeah," she said after a beat, her voice strained. "It's just—my dad."

"What's going on?"

Linda sighed deeply, running a hand through her hair, which only dislodged more strands from the bun. "He's...

not doing well. The doctors don't think he has much time left."

"Wait, what?"

"He's been sick for a while, you know," she reasoned. "But it's different now. You can just tell, you know? That... shift. My mom's doing her best, but she's exhausted, and I—I don't know how to split myself between work and home without feeling like I'm failing both."

"I didn't even know all of this was going on, Linda... wow. I... Honestly, I don't know if there's any version of this where you won't feel stretched thin."

Her laugh was short and humorless, and she shook her head, freeing another strand of hair. "And knowing that doesn't make it any easier."

I nodded, folding my arms. "You're not failing anyone, though. You're doing what you can, and that's enough. I promise you that it is."

She snorted softly, rubbing at her temple. "Easy to say. But when you're in it... I don't know. Do you ever feel like you're just one wrong move away from dropping the whole damn thing?"

I met her gaze, my voice steady but soft. "Every day."

Her eyes flicked to mine, surprised; for a moment, the tension in her shoulders eased just slightly.

I shrugged, the corner of my mouth tugging into a faint smile. "I don't have any big, wise advice for you; that's usually Caroline's thing. But I know this—your dad doesn't care if you're perfect. He just cares that you're there. If these... if these truly are his last moments, I'm sure all he wants is you close to him."

Linda's jaw tightened, and she nodded, blinking quickly as she pressed her lips together. "Yeah. You're right." Her voice cracked a little, but she didn't try to hide it this time. "I just... it's hard to know what to do. And it's hard to be brave, hold on, and be the strong face for everyone around you."

"I can only imagine..." I admitted, my own voice softer now. "You don't have to figure it all out at once. Start with what's in front of you. Today, it's this shift. Tomorrow, it's calling your mom or sitting with your dad. One thing at a time."

She exhaled deeply, and her shoulders dropped a little for the first time. "Thanks, Imara. I needed that."

I squeezed her arm gently, then let my hand fall away. "Anytime. And seriously, if you need time off or someone to cover for you, just say the word. You've got a whole team here."

Linda gave me a small, genuine smile, and it was enough to remind me why I came here in the first place.

CHAPTER 12: FADING VITALS

I leaned against the nurse's station, rubbing the back of my neck and suppressing a yawn. The last hour had dragged, and I could feel the day's weight settling into my shoulders like bricks.

"You look like you're about five minutes away from face-planting into the chart rack," Caroline teasingly said as she flipped through a clipboard.

"Not far off," I replied, stretching my arms overhead. "I'm officially done as soon as the clock hits, and trust me, I'm not sticking around a second longer."

Caroline grinned, tucking a stray curl behind her ear. "Night shift magic, huh? You sure you don't miss it?"

"Not in the slightest," I said with a laugh. "But you enjoy the chaos."

Before she could respond, the faint sound of frantic footsteps echoed down the hall. At first, it was subtle, like someone moving quickly, but then it grew louder: heels clicking against the linoleum, a distant voice shouting for help.

Caroline and I exchanged a glance and straightened instinctively.

"We need a doctor—now!"

Caroline and I locked eyes for half a second before we moved; my gloves snagged from the counter mid-step.

The stretcher burst through the double doors, paramedics flanking it like it was about to fall apart. One gripped the rail tightly, barking out vitals-like commands.

"Male, mid-sixties," the lead paramedic called out, his voice sharp and steady. "Post-op, possible internal bleed. BP's 78 and dropping! O2 at 82—unresponsive since we left the scene."

Another paramedic added, "We started oxygen in transit. He hasn't had an epi yet, but we've been bagging him to keep levels stable. There has been no change."

The patient's pale lips had a blue tinge. His chest rose in shallow, uneven bursts, every breath sounding like it was fighting and wrestling its way out of his lungs.

"Room 206," I said firmly, already running through the steps in my head.

"Get him on the bed—careful, watch the lines!" I barked, taking charge as the paramedics shifted him onto the mattress.

Monitors screamed, drowning out the shuffle of feet and the clatter of equipment. Caroline was at my side, her face tight with focus as she grabbed gloves from her pocket.

"IV's kinked," I muttered, my hands darting to the line. "Caroline, swap out the saline—he's dry."

"On it," she replied, already tearing into a fresh bag.

"BP's dropping—68 and falling!"

I glanced at the monitor, my stomach flipping at the jagged dips of his vitals. The EKG pads stuck awkwardly to his damp skin as a nurse fumbled to calibrate the machine.

"Bag him!" I shouted, reaching for the Ambu bag and snapping it into place. My hands moved instinctively, squeezing rhythmically, but my mind raced.

Where the hell is Dr. Whitaker? This wasn't exactly a drill.

"Pulse ox is 75 and dropping fast," one of the paramedics said, their voice sharp with urgency.

"Then let's stabilize it before this gets worse." I snapped back, my tone clipped as I kept bagging. "Caroline, get me a fresh line—16-gauge, left arm."

She nodded, tossing a packet onto the tray and ripping the old line free with practiced efficiency.

"Epi?" one of the nurses asked, hovering near the crash cart.

"No!" I shot back. "Not yet. This isn't cardiac—it's post-op. We stabilize pressure and O2 first, or we'll just mask the problem."

The room felt like it was shrinking. Monitors screamed. The crash cart rattled as a nurse bumped it in their hurry. My gloves stuck to my skin, and sweat gathered at my temples.

"Come on," I muttered, focusing on the patient's face. His chest rose shallowly, the effort etched into every line on his face. "You're not giving up on me yet."

Caroline tossed a glance my way. "Vitals still tanking. What's next?"

I tightened my grip on the Ambu bag. "We hold. Stabilize the line and recheck pressure in one minute."

The door slammed open, and Dr. Whitaker strode in like he was waltzing into rounds.

"Finally," I muttered under my breath, not missing the way Caroline smirked beside me.

"What's the situation?" he asked, scanning the room.

"Post-op, possible internal bleed," I replied sharply, not stopping my work. "BP's 68, pulse ox 75, and we're stabilizing fluids."

He didn't hesitate, stepping to the other side of the bed. His hazel eyes flicked to the line I was adjusting. "You should've started with a larger bore IV," he said in a tone that felt less suggestive and more like a statement.

I gritted my teeth, forcing my focus to stay on the task at hand. "I already swapped it out."

"Then why is the flow rate still so slow?" He countered, reaching across to check the connection himself.

"Because it's not the line—it's the patient," I snapped, shooting him a quick glare. "His pressure's too low to push faster without risking collapse."

His brow furrowed, and he opened his mouth to argue, but Caroline beat him to it.

"She's right," Caroline said, her tone sharp as she tossed another bag onto the tray. "We're working on stabilizing him first."

Sam's jaw tightened, but he didn't back down. "You're wasting time. Epi could've bought us a window."

"And crashed his system," I bit out, straightening as I finished securing the line. "We're not masking symptoms. We're fixing the problem."

"BP stabilizing!" Caroline called out, relief breaking through the chaos.

"75, 80, climbing," the paramedic added, their voice lifting.

I stepped back slightly, letting out a breath I didn't realize I was holding. My gloves came off with a snap, and I tossed them into the bin, my hands shaking slightly.

Sam watched me, his jaw tight as his hazel eyes flicked between me and the patient. "Epi would've been faster," he muttered loud enough for me to hear.

"And it would've masked the actual issue," I countered, meeting his gaze without flinching. "This was the right call. I'm sorry if you felt like I overstepped."

He didn't argue; he just nodded stiffly and turned to address the paramedics.

Caroline nodded, giving me a moment before speaking again. "What was that back there? He seemed a little... intense."

I huffed out a dry laugh, running a hand over my hair, still damp with sweat.

"He means well—he always does. But sometimes, I think he's so used to leading that he forgets how to step back."

Her lips twitched into a small smile. "That tracks. I mean, he's good at what he does. But I've noticed he likes to... refine things. Even when they don't need refining."

I nodded, my frustration ebbing as I let out a small sigh. "It's not a bad thing, usually. I appreciate his attention to detail—I really do. But in situations like this, when time is everything? It just rubs me the wrong way."

She tilted her head, her tone thoughtful. "You handled it well, though. You stood your ground."

"I had to," I said, shrugging. "It wasn't about me or him; it was about saving the patient's life. But it's not the first time. He'll chime in with suggestions when I'm halfway through something or double-check work that we're already doing. I know it's not personal, but..."

"It gets old," she finished, nodding.

"Yeah." I leaned against the counter, glancing back toward the closed door. "But it's not worth dwelling on. We saved the patient—that's what matters."

Caroline paused. "Are you going to talk to him?"

I glanced back toward the door. "I need to," I admitted. "I don't want this hanging over us. He's a good doctor, and we usually work well together most of the time. But if I don't say something, things might get... strained. And I don't want to ruin our working relationship or our friendship."

Caroline nodded slowly, a flicker of approval in her eyes. "That's fair. You're better than me, though. I'd probably just stew about it for a week."

I smirked, shaking my head. "Tempting. But I'd rather get ahead of it before it becomes a bigger deal."

"Well, when you do, don't hold back. He respects you, and you've earned it."

CHAPTER 13: LINGERING GLANCES

The clock read 7:45, but it felt more like 3 a.m. I stifled a yawn as I flipped through patient charts at the nurse's station, willing my brain to engage for just a few more hours and then... bliss.

Tomorrow was my first Sunday off in weeks, and the plan was to make it count with a steaming mug of tea, a warm blanket, and the trashiest show I could find to binge-watch. It had been so long since I'd indulged in doing absolutely nothing that I'd forgotten what it felt like. But I was ready to remember.

The thought alone was enough to put a small smile on my face. Then, I glanced up and spotted Dr. Whitaker disappearing into his office, his coffee in hand and his stride entirely too purposeful for this hour of the morning.

My smile faded, replaced by a pang of unresolved frustration.

Yesterday's exchange was still fresh in my mind, and it had been gnawing at me like an itch I couldn't scratch. I told Caroline I'd talk to him about it, and if I was going to rot on my couch tomorrow without this hanging over me, now was the time.

I grabbed the closest excuse for a clipboard, clutching it like a shield as I made my way to his office. The plan was simple: nip it in the bud, keep it professional, and then get on with my day.

But as I approached, I heard another voice coming from just inside.

"She's been incredible."

I froze mid-step, my knuckles hovering above the door. Through the small glass pane, I caught sight of Linda standing across from him, a clipboard in her hand, her head tilted as she listened.

"I told her about the program," Dr. Whitaker continued, his voice lowering ever so slightly, "and I think she'll be a great fit. She's exactly the kind of nurse we need."

My chest tightened as I stepped back, his words swirling in my mind. He's talking about me: praising me. Guilt prickled at the edges of my thoughts. A part of me felt cornered.

"Well, I can't argue with you on that. She's got the kind of game we haven't seen here in a while..." Linda's voice was as clear as day. "But do you think she's ready for something like this? You know how straining it can get—poor kid just got here."

"She's ready," he said without hesitation, the conviction in his voice enough to make my chest tighten. "She might not see it yet, but she is."

"Let's face it, Sam—you have a way of leaning in real hard when you're all in on something."

Whitaker's laugh came quick, a quiet rumble that barely lasted. "Not pushing. Guiding."

"Is that what we're calling it now?"

"She doesn't even know how good she is yet," Whitaker said, quieter this time, like he was talking to himself more than Linda.

"Just don't push her, Sam. Not everyone likes being steered, even if you think you're doing it gently."

I swallowed hard, the lump in my throat refusing to budge. She was not wrong. And the fact that she was even saying it meant she'd also noticed it.

I took a deep breath and stepped into the office. His gaze lifted immediately, catching mine like it had been waiting for me all along. The stiffness in his posture melted, replaced by something softer and warmer. His lips curled into an easy smile, which eased my worries just a bit.

"Imara! Speak of the devil," he said with a grin. "I was just speaking with Linda about you."

I forced a small smile, stepped further inside, and let the door click shut behind me. "So I heard."

His grin faltered for a fraction of a second, his brow twitching as he tilted his head. "Ah. Right."

I glanced at the chair across from his desk but didn't sit; I kept the clipboard tucked under my arm like it was holding me up. "I wanted to talk to you, actually."

He straightened his hands and folded them loosely on the desk. "Of course. What's on your mind?"

I hesitated, shifting my weight as I glanced at the corner of the room, avoiding his eyes. It's one thing to plan the conversation in my head and another to have it.

"I appreciate everything you've done for me since I got here," I started, the words measured, careful. "The guidance, the support; it hasn't gone unnoticed."

"But?" he prompted, his voice soft but direct as if he knew exactly where this was going.

"But," I echoed, finally meeting his gaze, "sometimes it feels like... you're hovering."

He blinked, sitting back in his chair. "Hovering?"

"Yes." The word came out firmer than I had intended, but I didn't back down. "I know you mean well, but there are moments—like yesterday—when it feels like you don't trust me to make the right call."

Whitaker exhaled slowly, his fingers tapping once against the desk before he realized and stopped himself. "Imara, that's not—"

"I know it's not intentional," I interrupted, my voice steady but not unkind. "But it's there. And I need you to understand that I can capably make good decisions in the heat of the moment without someone second-guessing me."

His lips pressed into a thin line, his gaze steady on mine. "Yesterday was a tense situation. I wasn't second-guessing you—I was trying to make sure we didn't lose the patient."

"And we didn't," I replied, my tone calm but pointed. "Because I made the right call. And if you'd trusted me from the start, we wouldn't even be having this conversation."

For a moment, the room was silent, the air thick with the weight of the exchange. His shoulders dropped slightly, the tension in his posture giving way to something almost resigned.

Whitaker nodded slowly, his gaze dropping to the desk momentarily before it met mine again. "Fair enough. I'll work on it. But, for the record..." He leaned forward slightly, a small, rueful smile tugging at his lips. "I wasn't kidding when I told Linda you've been incredible. I meant every word."

"Thank you. I've had a wonderful time working here."

Dr. Whitaker leaned back in his chair, studying me for a moment. His smile softened, and for a beat, I thought we were done and I could walk out of there with everything said and squared away.

"While I have you here," he began. "I've got a drive for the outreach program this afternoon. Maybe it'll persuade you a bit more to see what it's all about."

"This afternoon?"

"Yep." He stood and grabbed his keys, spinning them lightly on his finger. "No time like the present. Unless you've got other plans?"

My eyes darted to the framed degrees on the wall, the neatly stacked folders on his desk, and anything but the eager look on his face.

It was hard to say no, especially after how receptive he was to everything I'd just said.

I let out a small breath, giving a reluctant smile. "Alright. Let's do it."

"Excellent choice," he said with a grin, motioning for me to follow him out of the office. As we passed the nurses' station, he tossed a quick word to Linda and Caroline, letting them know we'd be out for a bit.

Caroline raised an eyebrow, her lips curving into a knowing smirk as her gaze flickered between us. "Enjoy your little adventure," she teased, her voice in a singsong as she waved me off.

I rolled my eyes and followed him out. The sun was out, but it didn't do much against the sharp bite of the wind. His Subaru Outback was clean, practical, and just... normal. It suited him.

The first few minutes of the drive were quiet, only the low hum of the engine and the sight of the town slowly giving way to snow-dusted fields and dense pine forests.

"You know, I grew up in a neighborhood where... well, let's just say most people didn't end up amounting to much. Resources were scarce, and opportunities were even scarcer. It wasn't just poverty—it was the complete absence of care. No one believed in us. No one invested in us."

"I was lucky," he said after a pause. "I had a teacher who refused to give up on me. She saw something in me when I didn't even see it in myself. She'd stay after school to tutor me and pull strings to get me into programs not meant for kids from my zip code. She saved my life in more ways than one."

"Is that why you started the outreach program?" I asked as I watched his profile.

His gaze flickered to me briefly, a faint smile tugging at the corners of his lips. "Yeah. I figured it would be worth it if I could do a fraction of what she did for me. It's about reaching people who've gone overlooked and communities where access to healthcare, education, and basic necessities is a privilege instead of a right."

His hands relaxed on the steering wheel, his thumbs brushing over it absently as he continued. "We offer free health clinics, partner with local organizations to provide resources, and try to create pathways for people to get the help they need. It's not perfect, but it's something."

I glanced out the window, watching the trees blur past in shades of winter gray, and tried to figure out what to say to someone who seemed to have all the right answers.

"You don't think small, do you?"

He chuckled at that, a low sound that was almost self-conscious. "Guess not. But you'd be surprised what a little ambition can do."

I turned back to him, my fingers brushing the hem of my scarf as I studied his face. The faint lines at the corners of his eyes, the way his jaw tightened every now and then when he talked about it.

"Ambition," I repeated, testing the word on my tongue. "And exhaustion, I imagine."

"Definitely," he agreed. "But it's necessary. And the truth is, it's personal. I see myself in some of the people we help, especially the kids who only need someone to believe in them and families who deserve more than they receive. It's not perfect, but it's something."

"I don't think I've ever let myself think that way," I admitted. "My whole life's been about checking the boxes— school, nursing, saving up, getting married, building the white picket fence. That was the plan. Perfect on paper."

"But something like this... building something that actually feeds your soul? I don't think I've ever asked myself what that would look like, let alone tried to pour myself into it."

"Hey... I swear it's not always as noble as it sounds. Most days, it's messy and frustrating. You pour your heart into something, and it feels like you're getting nowhere. Like you're trying to bail out the ocean with a bucket."

"But," he continued, "now and then, you see that it's working. Even if it's just a tiny ripple, and it reminds you why you started. It's never too late."

The outreach program took us to Peacham, Vermont. Sam navigated the winding roads like he'd done it a hundred times before; before long, we were at a community center.

I spotted a small but bustling scene as we pulled into the parking lot. The building was modest, but I could see a makeshift clinic with folding tables and chairs arranged in neat rows. Volunteers in warm jackets and scarves moved between cars in the lot, directing people where to go and carrying boxes of supplies.

"This is it," Sam said, parking the car. "Welcome to Peacham's monthly outreach clinic."

We got out of the car and stepped inside; the warmth of the space was a welcome contrast to the crisp chill outside. The clinic hummed with activity. A line of patients checked in at a table near the entrance, greeted by cheerful volunteers. Further back, I saw a small corner set up for kids, complete with coloring books and crayons.

"Morning, Dr. Whitaker!" called out a young man stacking medical kits by the wall.

"Morning, Andy," Sam called out, his tone light and familiar as he approached a stocky EMT unloading supplies from his bag. "How's Sophie? Did she break into a run yet?"

Andy's head snapped up, his grin immediate. "Walking like she owns the place. It's the wobble that gets you, though— she's got no idea how close she comes to face-planting half the time."

"Classic," Sam replied, nodding like he'd been there before. "Next thing you know, she'll figure out stairs, and that's when the real fun begins."

"Don't remind me," Andy groaned, slinging the bag over his shoulder. His gaze shifted to me, curious but friendly. "Hey, I don't think we've met. New recruit?"

"She's with me," Sam answered before I could speak. "Andy, meet Imara. Imara, this is Andy—the most efficient EMT in the state and a former star of our outreach program."

Andy chuckled, scratching the back of his neck. "I wouldn't go that far, but yeah, they got me through certification. Saved my ass back when I was... let's just say, figuring life out."

I blinked at him, taken off guard. He looked like he'd always had it together: calm, confident, the kind of guy who never breaks a sweat.

"The program helped you?"

"Big time," he said, his smile turning a little sheepish. "Got me on track after Sophie was born. I was, uh, eighteen at the time."

Sam grinned, leaning against the wall. I could tell he never got tired of hearing it. "And now he's one of the best in the business."

"Thanks to this guy," Andy added, gesturing toward Sam before hoisting his bag higher. "Anyway, I gotta set up. Nice to meet you, Imara."

"You too," I said distantly as I watched him disappear down the hallway.

Sam cleared his throat, pulling my attention back to him. "So, here's the layout," he said, all business now. "We've got basic checkups and immunizations at the first station." He pointed toward a table with a line already forming. "The nutritionist's over there." Another nod toward a display of pamphlets and plastic fruit. "And there's a counselor taking appointments in the next room."

Sam led me to a small station tucked into the corner, where a volunteer was carefully unpacking a blood pressure cuff. She glanced up as we approached, pushing her glasses higher on her nose, and smiled warmly.

"Imara," Sam said, gesturing toward her. "Meet Darlene. She's been with the program since before I even knew what I was doing."

Darlene snorted, standing and wiping her hands on her jeans before extending one to me. "Don't let him fool you. He still doesn't know what he's doing half the time."

"Harsh," Sam quipped, holding a hand to his chest like she'd wounded him.

I stifled a laugh as I took her hand. Her grip was firm, her knuckles dusted with faint freckles, and her knit hat was slightly askew over her dark curls. "Nice to meet you," I said, glancing at the neatly arranged supplies on the table. "It looks like you've got this down to a science."

"Decades of practice," she said, her smile widening. "Though you never stop learning in this line of work. How long have you been a nurse?"

"Just over a year and a half," I replied, pulling my coat tighter as a draft swept through the room. "First time doing something like this, though."

"Well, stick with me, and you'll be fine. This is less intimidating than it looks."

Sam grinned, stepping back. "You're in good hands. Darlene's the best." He winked at her, and she waved him off like he was embarrassing her, but the warmth in her expression lingered.

For the next few hours, I worked alongside Darlene, assisting patients who ranged from hesitant to chatty. We took blood pressure, handed out pamphlets, and answered medication questions.

The supply table was bustling: Darlene was handing out pamphlets, volunteers were restocking formula cans, and someone was laughing too loudly a few feet away. But a woman near the back of the room caught my attention.

She was standing by the wall, her shoulders pulled tight, clutching her coat like it might slip away. The baby strapped to her chest let out a soft whimper, but she barely noticed, her gaze fixed on the supply table with the intensity of someone debating whether to bolt or step forward.

I glanced at Darlene, who was preoccupied with a stack of forms, then stepped toward the woman, weaving through the clusters of people between us. As I got closer, she looked up, startled, and her grip on the baby carrier strap tightened.

"Hi," I said softly, stopping just short of her personal space. "Do you need some help?"

Her eyes, wide and uncertain, flicked to mine. She nodded but didn't speak, her fingers digging into the worn fabric of her coat.

"It can be overwhelming," I continued, keeping my tone easy. "But we're here to help. That's what this is for." I nodded toward the table, where volunteers were handing out cans of formula and diapers like clockwork.

"I don't know, he's having a hard time breastfeeding, but..." she said finally, her voice barely audible. "I don't want to take too much. Someone else might need it more."

"You need it," I said simply, gesturing toward the baby, who was now fussing against her chest. "I can't imagine going home tonight, knowing you walked out of here without anything to feed him. I wouldn't sleep."

What would it feel like? To go home, to have a baby and not know how to care for them—how to feed them? The thought alone was enough to send a shiver down my spine, and I swallowed hard against the knot forming in my throat.

Before she could respond, a voice cut in behind me. "She's right."

I turned to see Sam approaching, his hands in his pockets and his expression calm but resolute. "You don't have to justify needing help," he added, his gaze steady on the woman. "That's what we're here for."

Her eyes darted between us, her unease palpable. "I just... I don't want to be greedy."

"You're not," Sam said firmly, stepping closer. "You're a mom doing what's best for your baby. That's not greedy— that's brave...that's responsible."

Her lips trembled, and I watched her jaw tighten like she was trying to hold herself together.

"How old is he?" I asked, nodding toward the baby.

"Two months," she whispered, glancing down at him like she was double-checking.

"Two months?" Sam's tone lightened, his smile soft. "That's a tough age. I bet you're not getting much sleep, huh?"

She shook her head, a small, tired laugh slipping out. "Not really."

"That's even more reason to take what you need," I said, keeping my voice low. "Let us make things just a little easier, even if it's just for today."

Her eyes flicked back to Sam, who nodded toward the table. "Formula, diapers, wipes—they're all there for you. And if you need anything else, just let us know."

She hesitated, her gaze lingering on the table. Then, slowly, she stepped forward.

As Darlene greeted her with a kind smile and started gathering supplies, I glanced at Sam, who was watching the woman with a quiet focus.

"You've got a way with words," I said under my breath.

Sam's smile tilted into something faintly self-deprecating. "It's not words. It's people. You just meet them where they are."

When I lost the baby, no one knew how to meet me there. Not really. They said things like, "You're young, you'll have another chance," and "Everything happens for a reason." All those well-meaning clichés that just made the ache sharper.

What would it have been like, I wondered, to have someone say something real? Or maybe not say anything at all—just sit there, hold my hand, and remind me I didn't have to carry it alone. Someone like Sam, maybe. A good friend.

I wanted to say something—maybe agree, maybe push back—but the young mother turned back to us, clutching a canister of formula like it was a lifeline.

"Thank you," she said softly, her voice trembling. "Really, thank you."

Sam nodded, his hands still in his pockets. "You've got this," he said simply.

I watched her disappear into the crowd, the baby letting out a soft coo.

"I'll do it," I muttered, the words slipping out before I even realized I'd said them.

"What was that?" Sam's voice pulled me back. I swiped at my eyes with the back of my hand, pretending it was just the cold air drifting in every time the door opened.

"I'll join the program, Dr. Whitaker."

CHAPTER 14: PERSONAL SPACES

Sunday. The cup of tea was warm against my palms, the heat seeping into my skin as the faint curl of steam brushed against my face. I brought it close, letting the warmth spread through me in slow, deliberate waves.

As my eyes wandered around the apartment, waiting for the Timeless TV app to load, I caught a glimpse of my reflection in the hallway mirror.

I stopped, tilting my head as I took in the faint shimmer of morning light hitting my face. My pixie cut was starting to grow out, and the soft curls were brushing just past my ears. I reached up, smoothing a stray curl back into place and letting my fingers linger for a moment.

"Should I let it grow?" I muttered, tilting my head to the other side, considering.

The thought felt silly as soon as it surfaced, and I laughed quietly, shaking my head. "Not likely," I murmured, running a hand through the short layers.

The dark circles under my eyes had faded to some degree, and there was a bit of color in my cheeks again. My brown skin glowed softly in the morning light, and for once, I didn't look completely worn down.

"Well, hey there, stranger."

My smile faltered slightly when my gaze drifted past my reflection and into the room behind me. It had neutral-toned walls and plain curtains.

A small, unexpected thrill shot through me, and I took a long sip of tea, trying to contain it. But the gears in my head were already spinning, clanking together with ideas and possibilities.

I carefully set the mug down, the ceramic clicking against the coaster. Then, without giving myself a chance to second-guess, I grabbed my keys from the counter, my slippers barely clinging to my feet as I headed for the door.

"Alright, let's do this."

The store greeted me with its signature mix of overwhelming possibility and mild chaos. It was the kind of place you walked into with a plan and walked out of with an identity crisis—and a cart full of things you didn't know you needed.

First, a roll of removable wallpaper in a soft botanical print caught my eye. Then, there was a set of twinkle lights, a quirky vase shaped like a pair of rain boots, and a stack of cozy throw pillows in varying shades of mustard yellow and deep green.

I passed by a display of scented candles and immediately slowed down. Someone had lined them up like miniature trophies, each one daring me to find the one that'd single-handedly fix my life. I scanned the labels quickly: Cozy Chaos, Flannel Fantasy, and—oh, wow—Sweater Weather with a Side of Regret.

That one stopped me in my tracks. I picked it up, turning the jar over in my hands, the corners of my mouth twitching. Vanilla, cedarwood, and... questionable decisions? Yep, that tracked. I tossed it into the cart before I could second-guess myself, muttering, "Might as well lean into the theme."

A nearby shopper glanced at me, her brow slightly furrowed, and I cleared my throat, quickly grabbing another candle labeled Haunted Hygge to look busy.

Beside me, a child shrieked delightfully as their parent begrudgingly agreed to a Halloween-themed kitchen towel. Across the way, two teenagers took selfies with a life-sized inflatable reindeer.

I turned the corner and almost knocked over a small pyramid of framed art prints. One caught my eye: a simple illustration of a bird perched on a branch, its wings mid-flutter. I added it to the pile without hesitation.

By the time I reached the cashier, my cart was a colorful, chaotic mess of items that didn't exactly match but somehow fit together in my mind. The cashier raised an eyebrow as she rang me up, her expression equal parts amused and curious.

"Big project?" she asked, scanning the bird print.

"Something like that," I replied with a grin.

I paid, and while I was pushing my cart toward the automatic doors, I was distracted, mentally arranging where everything would go in my apartment. The wallpaper behind the couch will be perfect, and the twinkle lights along the window will be perfect.

I didn't notice him until it was too late.

"Oof!" I stumbled backward, barely catching myself as my cart jerked to a stop. A tall figure loomed in front of me, equally thrown off balance. My hands gripped the cart tightly as I looked up, and my breath caught.

He was tall—really tall—and his dark skin seemed to glow under the store's lights. He had sharp features, a strong jawline, full lips, and intensity in his eyes as he glanced down at me. But just as I was about to open my mouth to apologize, his gaze dropped back to the phone pressed against his ear.

"Yeah, yeah, I'm working on it," he grumbled into the receiver. "I get it, alright? Just handle the morning shift until I can sort this out."

His words tumbled out in a rush, his tone clipped, and without another glance at me, he strode away, one hand gripping a reusable shopping bag, the other gesturing animatedly as he continued his call.

I blinked, stunned, my apology stuck in my throat. Did he just—?

"Unbelievable," I muttered under my breath, brushing myself off. My gaze lingered on his retreating figure for a moment, a part of me registering how handsome he was. But the rest of me bristled at the lack of basic decency.

Shaking my head, I pushed my cart out to the parking lot. The cool air hit my face and snapped me back to reality.

By the time I got home, the interaction had already been pushed to the back of my mind, replaced by the excitement of decorating. I spent the next few hours transforming my apartment into something that felt like... well, me.

The botanical wallpaper went up first, and I paid extra attention to smoothing out every wrinkle. The twinkle lit the window frame perfectly, their soft glow instantly making the space feel warmer.

I even found a spot for the bird print, hanging it just above the bookshelf I stocked with novels I'd barely touched since moving in.

Once done, I collapsed onto the couch, the pile of throw pillows cushioning me like a nest. I glanced around the room, pride swelling in my chest. Every corner of this space reflected something I loved and had chosen.

My gaze lingered on the botanical wallpaper behind the couch, the one I almost didn't buy. It reminded me of my mom's old garden—rows of herbs and flowers she'd tended to with care, no matter how busy life got. My chest tightened, a bittersweet ache settling in. She'd love this space. She'd tell me to send her pictures so she could gush about it to her friends.

I hadn't spoken to them in weeks, and I hadn't let them know that I was okay—or at least starting to be. My hand drifted to my phone on the armrest, and I picked it up before I could talk myself out of it.

My thumbs hovered over the keyboard as I tried to figure out how to start.

Hey, Mom and Dad. Vermont is... interesting. The work is fine, and the people are nice. I even decorated my apartment—

I stopped, deleting the words. What was I supposed to say? That I missed them? That I felt lonelier than I expected, but also kind of... good? Should I tell them that I'd found something here I didn't even know I was looking for?

I bit my lip, staring at the empty text box before locking my phone and setting it down on the coffee table. Maybe tomorrow.

CHAPTER 15: HI STRANGER

I stepped into the hospital, the warmth hitting me like a hug after the biting cold outside. My boots squeaked against the tile floor and announced my arrival before I had a chance to shake the snow off my coat.

I stopped mid-step, frowning as I glanced over my shoulder. "Uh... is there a fire? Did someone code?"

Before she could answer, Caroline rounded the corner, her arms full of charts, moving with all the urgency of someone late for something important. But the second she spotted me, she froze. The charts tilted precariously in her arms as she stared—no, glared at me, wide-eyed.

"Oh, sweet baby Jesus. It's worse than I thought," she muttered, her gaze drifting down to my feet like they'd personally offended her.

"What is?" I asked, genuinely confused.

Linda stepped closer, arms crossed, her expression one of pure, unfiltered disappointment.

"Imara, we've been patient. We've been kind."

I blinked. "What are you talking about?"

"Two weeks, Imara," Caroline chimed in, stepping closer with an exaggerated shiver. "Two weeks of you showing up to work dressed like you're ready to fight the Arctic in nothing but thin rags and sheer determination. Do you even own a proper winter coat?"

Linda gestured at my boots—the ones I'd been trudging around in since I got here. They were scuffed, slightly damp around the edges, and entirely unremarkable.

"And those," she said, as if the word itself was an insult. "Those sad excuses for boots."

Caroline gasped, her expression one of mock horror. "Oh no, Linda, don't look too long. They might hurt your soul."

I stared down at my feet, baffled. "What's wrong with my boots? They're fine!"

"Fine?" Linda echoed, her voice dripping with disbelief. "Imara, those boots wouldn't survive a puddle, let alone a Vermont winter. How have they not disintegrated on you already?"

Caroline stepped forward, her tone conspiratorial. "But be honest. Did you bring those here as some sort of tribute to Florida or something?"

I bit back a laugh. "I'm not from Florida."

"Could've fooled us," Linda quipped, her eyes narrowing. "Those boots scream, 'I've never seen snow before in my life.'"

"Alright, alright," I said, throwing my hands up. "I get it. My boots are a tragedy. Happy?"

Linda grinned, clearly pleased with herself. "Ecstatic. Now, do yourself a favor and go get some real ones before you lose a toe."

Caroline patted me on the shoulder as she passed by, her sing-song voice being as remarkable as it had always been. "She's just looking out for you, sweetie. We all are."

As they walked away, their laughter echoing down the hallway, I glanced down at my boots again. Okay, so maybe they were not the most Vermont-appropriate footwear. But did they really deserve that kind of roasting?

The thought lingered in my mind all morning, their playful jabs replaying every time I passed by the nurse's station and caught their smug grins. By lunchtime, I'd made up my mind.

These boots had got to go.

I stood outside the local boutique, my breath fogging in the cold air as I stared at the display window. The attendants had arranged the rows of boots in neat, inviting lines, and I felt a little overwhelmed as I stepped inside.

The store was cozy, and the air scented faintly of leather and cedar. I wandered the aisles, taking in the options: practical snow boots with thick soles and sleek leather ones that looked more suited for city sidewalks than snowdrifts. It was a lot to take in.

After a few minutes, I felt stuck. On one hand, there was a sturdy black pair—practical, warm, and utterly boring. On the other, a tan suede pair lined with faux fur that was completely adorable, but it screamed "bad decisions."

I picked up one of each, holding them up like I was conducting a very serious interrogation. "Alright," I muttered, "which one of you wants to come home with me?"

"You'd better not pick the tan ones," a voice interjected, crisp and unwavering, with just the faintest trace of amusement.

I whipped my head around, startled. A petite woman stood a few feet away, her pixie-cut hair perfectly styled, every strand seemingly in its rightful place. She had crossed her arms and arched one brow, giving me a look that felt both deeply judgmental and oddly... charming.

"They're hideous," she added, her lips twitching upward as if she was holding back a smile.

I glanced down at the tan boots, then back up at her. "Hideous?"

"They'll betray you the second they see snow," she continued, crossing her arms. "Trust me, you don't want that kind of drama in your life."

For a second, I just stared, unsure whether to laugh or be offended. "Drama?"

"Oh, absolutely. Those boots are liars. Pretty liars, but liars all the same." She nodded toward the black pair in my other hand. "Now, these? These will have your back. Dependable. Classic. No nonsense."

Her tone was so matter-of-fact that I found myself nodding along before I even realized it. "I... guess you have a point."

"I always do," she said lightly, her lips quirking into a small smile. "But don't let me stop you from making a terrible decision. It builds character. I just expect someone with the same hairstyle as me to have a better fashion sense."

I chuckled, shaking my head as I set the tan boots back on the shelf. "I'll stick with dependable."

"Smart girl," she said, her approval obvious as she stepped past me to grab a scarf from a nearby rack. She tossed it over her shoulder with a flourish before turning back. "And get yourself a good scarf while you're at it. If you're going to survive Vermont, you'll need all the help you can get."

"I'll take that under advisement," I managed, shaking my head.

She smirked, clearly pleased with herself. "Good. Someone has to keep you on the right track."

We fell into step as she examined a nearby rack of gloves. "So, you're not from here, are you?" she asked, glancing at me knowingly.

"Is it that obvious?"

"Painfully." She grinned. "But don't worry; I'm not judging. Vermont isn't exactly an easy place to adjust to. I've been here for years and still don't get along with most people."

I raised an eyebrow, intrigued. "That bad?"

"Let's just say Vermonters have their quirks," she said lightly, holding up a pair of bright yellow mittens with a critical eye. "But you seem decent enough. You're not going to, I don't know, start lecturing me on maple syrup purity or something, are you?"

"Not unless it's part of my Vermont initiation," I joked.

She laughed, the sound light and carefree, and stuck out her hand. "Charlotte."

"Imara," I replied, shaking her hand. Her grip was firm but friendly, and something about her energy felt... easy, like she was exactly who she seemed to be.

"Well, Imara, welcome to Vermont. Let me know if you need a crash course on surviving the locals."

"I might take you up on that," I admitted, smiling.

She pulled her phone out of her pocket, her nails painted a deep burgundy. "Here, give me your number. If you're sticking around, you'll need someone to show you the ropes—and keep you from buying hideous boots."

I laughed again, typing my number into her phone. "Thanks. I'll take all the help I can get."

"Good. We'll start small with boots today and maybe a decent jacket next week."

As she headed toward the checkout, she glanced back over her shoulder. "Hang in there, new girl. Vermont grows on you. Eventually."

"I'm learning that already." I watched her go, a smile tugging at my lips.

As I stepped out into the cold with my new boots in hand, I realized I was looking forward to hearing from her again.

I pulled into my driveway, the heater in the car still blasting to fight off the cold that seemed to settle into my bones no matter how many layers I wore. Maybe Charlotte and I could bump jacket shopping up to this week.

My boots sat in the passenger seat, still tucked neatly in their box, and I couldn't help but glance at them with a little pride. It was a small thing, but it felt like a win.

A sharp voice followed the crunch of snow beneath my boots as I stepped out into the icy air.

"Miss Hastings!"

I turned to see Mr. Thompson, my neighbor from two houses down, standing at the edge of his driveway.

He was bundled into a heavy coat, his scarf tucked so tightly around his neck that it looked like it might strangle him. His face was as pinched as ever, his brows drawn into what seemed to be their permanent scowl.

"Yes, Mr. Thompson?" I asked, already bracing myself for whatever complaint he was about to lob my way.

He gestured vaguely toward my yard, his mittened hand waving like he was conducting an invisible orchestra. "Your snow," he said, his tone accusatory. "It keeps blowing into my driveway. Makes it a pain to keep it clear."

"My snow?"

"Yes, your snow," he snapped, as though I'd personally instructed the wind to inconvenience him. "Every time I finish shoveling, there it is again. Don't know why you can't just keep it in your own yard."

Its absurdity almost made me laugh, but I bit my tongue. Instead, I took a deep breath and nodded. "Alright, Mr. Thompson. I'll help clear it up."

That stopped him in his tracks. His scowl faltered, and he looked at me like I'd just spoken a foreign language. "You will?"

"Yes," I said simply, grabbing the shovel and leaning against the side of my house. "It'll only take a minute."

I made my way over to the invisible line where my yard ended and his began, the shovel digging into the snow with a satisfying crunch. Mr. Thompson watched, his arms crossed, as though he was waiting for me to change my mind. But I didn't.

I cleared the edge of his driveway and a bit beyond, tossing the snow neatly to the side. It was not much, but it was enough to stop the wind from blowing it back toward him— hopefully.

When I straightened up, my breath puffing out in clouds, he cleared his throat. "Well, uh... thank you," he muttered, clearly unused to saying the words. "That's decent of you."

"Anytime, Mr. Thompson," I replied, leaning the shovel back against the side of the house.

As I headed inside, shaking the snow off my boots at the door, I couldn't help but smile. It was a small thing, but it felt like a step forward. I'd take the little wins where I could get them.

CHAPTER 16: THAWING

I immediately sensed something was off the instance I walked into Ms. Carter's room. She was propped up against her pillows, her knitting needles resting idly in her lap instead of moving like a blur through some brightly colored yarn. Her expression was softer today, and her usually sharp wit was dulled.

"Good morning, Ms. Carter. How are we feeling today?"

She let out a small sigh, shifting slightly. "Oh, you know… achy. Tired. And this coffee they brought me might as well be dishwater."

There was no playful edge, no pointed jab lurking beneath the words. It was flat and subdued, as if she was struggling to speak through a heavy fog she couldn't quite push away.

I stepped closer, scanning her vitals as something uneasy tugged at the back of my mind. Her blood pressure was lower than I'd like, and her pulse was also slower. But it was the way she looked that really made my chest tighten.

Her skin, which was usually glowing with that unmistakable liveliness she carried even on her crankiest days, seemed dull, as if someone had turned the vibrance down a notch.

There was a faint sheen of sweat at her temple, and her scarf, which is always perfectly tied, was slipping slightly, the edges fraying against her neck.

I glanced at the chart, making a quick note to adjust her medication dosage. But it felt insufficient, like the chart and numbers couldn't possibly capture the quiet exhaustion etched into her face. Her eyes, which were normally brimming with that sharp, no-nonsense glint, looked dimmer and heavier.

"Have you been sleeping okay?" I asked, gently pressing the back of my hand to her forehead.

"Like a baby," she murmured, her lips quirking into a faint smile. "But not the good kind. The kind that wakes you up every two hours for no reason."

That got a small smile out of me, though it didn't do much to ease my concern. "All right, let's get you sorted out," I said, my voice firmer now as I focused on checking her IV line. "I'm going to tweak your meds a bit to help with the pain, okay?"

It was worrying that the medication didn't seem to be doing enough—not after everything we'd adjusted last time.

"Do what you've gotta do, darling," she said, her eyes closing as she leaned back against the pillows. "Just don't let them mess with my breakfast tomorrow. I've got a reputation to maintain."

That flicker of sass lightened the air, but as I stepped out of her room, my worry lingered. I tracked down Dr. Whitaker in his office, figuring it was best to get a second opinion.

I found him leaning back in his chair, a tablet balanced on his knee like he'd been there for hours. When I knocked lightly on the doorframe, he looked up, a small, easy smile spreading across his face.

"Imara," he said, setting the tablet down so fast it wobbled on the desk. "Don't tell me you're here to keep me company? Today's been oddly slow."

I stepped inside, the file tucked tightly under my arm. "Not quite, Sam. It's Ms. Carter. She's just... not herself today. Her vitals are off, and she's in more pain than usual. I adjusted her medication, but I wanted to run it by you."

He nodded, listening carefully, his expression thoughtful but calm as I went through the details. When I finished, he leaned forward, resting his elbows on the desk, his fingers steepled together like he was weighing my words.

"You did the right thing upping the dosage," he said, reassuring. "Chronic pain management for patients like Mrs. Carter—especially with her rheumatoid arthritis and the nerve damage in her lower back—is more about balance than perfection. Frustrating as they are, fluctuations like this can be normal, but it doesn't mean you're not on the right track."

I nodded, relief and doubt wrestling for control in my chest. "It would. I just didn't want to miss anything."

"You won't," he said with certainty, his tone leaving no room for argument. "Good instincts, though. Keep trusting those."

Even though his confidence was a little overwhelming at times, the encouragement felt genuine.

"What are you doing tonight?"

I blinked, thrown off balance. "Tonight?" I repeated, my voice sharper than I intended.

"Yes. I thought maybe we could grab a drink after work. You know, unwind a little."

Unwind?

My brain stuttered to process the words, and before I could stop it, panic flared in my chest.

Is he... asking me out?

My stomach tightened at the thought, and I must have looked like a deer caught in headlights because, just as I was fumbling for a response, he quickly waved a hand.

"Oh, and Linda and Caroline will be there too," he said, the words tumbling out of him a bit too fast. His fingers drummed lightly against the edge of his desk, a nervous habit I had started to pick up on. "It's something we all do now and then. No big deal."

My shoulders relaxed a fraction, the tension easing as I let out a shaky laugh. "Well, if Linda and Caroline are involved, I guess it's safe enough."

"Exactly," he said, a grin sliding into place like he never missed a beat. "I mean, unless you hate fun. But I wouldn't peg you for that."

A tiny smile tugged at my lips despite myself. "Drinks aren't exactly high on my to-do list these days."

"Well, they should be," he fired back easily. "You've been here long enough to need a break. Come on. It's harmless. Besides, Caroline's been sitting on a story about Linda for weeks—guaranteed to be worth it."

I hesitated, still trying to reconcile the smooth-talking doctor with the man who handed me his coffee without a second thought. His energy felt easy and genuine, but something about it also felt dangerous. Not in a bad way—more like a tightrope, but I don't know how to walk.

"Alright," I said finally, rolling my eyes. "But only because I want to see Linda squirm."

He chuckled, grabbing his coat from the back of his chair. "You won't regret it."

I snorted as I headed toward the door, glancing back at him with a smirk. "That's what everyone says before they make a bad decision."

"Maybe," he shot back, his grin lopsided. "But I don't think you'll be disappointed."

The bar wasn't what I expected. When I heard the word "bar," I pictured dim lighting, sticky counters, and overpriced drinks that tasted like regret. But this place was... cozy. It had warm wood accents, low golden lighting, and a chalkboard menu boasting things like "Berry Bliss

Mocktails" and "Mango Tango Smoothies." It was relaxed, almost quaint, and a far cry from the bustling chaos I'd been doing my best to avoid since I got here.

We snagged a small booth near the corner, and Caroline immediately slid in beside me, her eyes lighting up as she scanned the menu. "Okay, Imara, you have to try the Strawberry Sunrise. It's life-changing."

Linda raised an eyebrow from across the table. "You say that about everything, Caroline."

"Because I have impeccable taste," Caroline retorted, sticking her tongue out like a child. I laughed despite myself, and the sound surprised me. It felt easy here; I could let my guard down just a little.

Sam slid into the seat next to Linda. His broad shoulders looked slightly out of place in the small booth, but he seemed comfortable and at ease. He looked up and grinned as if sensing my glance, and I quickly averted my gaze, pretending to study the menu.

"Alright, team," Caroline declared, tapping the table with her fingertips. "The first round of drinks is on me, but only because I'm still high on the spirit of camaraderie or whatever."

Linda snorted. "Translation: She's trying to distract us so we don't bring up her patient who 'threw off her aura' again today."

Caroline gasped dramatically, clutching her chest. "How dare you!"

The teasing continued a back-and-forth that was so natural I almost forgot I was new there. Almost. But then, Linda's gaze flicked toward me, and her expression softened. "What about you, Imara? You've been awfully quiet."

Before I could respond, Caroline jumped in. "Yeah, don't let us monopolize the fun. You're part of the crew now, which automatically means you have to spill something. A fun fact, a deep secret, a slightly embarrassing childhood story—we don't discriminate."

I laughed nervously, shifting in my seat. "I'm not sure I have anything exciting to share."

"Come on," Sam said, his tone playful but his eyes attentive. "You can't be this mysterious forever. It's not allowed."

I hesitated, my fingers fidgeting with the edge of my napkin. "Well, I guess…"

My words trailed off when I glanced toward the bar. A tall figure stood at the counter, his broad back to me as he placed an order. Something about the casual way he leaned against the counter, his posture relaxed yet commanding, felt oddly familiar. He wore a dark coat, the collar turned up against the chill, and his voice carried just enough for me to catch a snippet of his order.

I couldn't place him, but the feeling nagged at me. Before I could dwell on it, Caroline nudged me with her elbow, pulling me back to the conversation. "Hello? Earth to Imara. Don't think I didn't see you zoning out. Do you know that guy?"

"No. I just... thought I recognized him. Anyway, what were we talking about?"

Caroline narrowed her eyes, clearly not buying it. "We were talking about how the mysterious act has got to go if you intend to stick around."

I groaned, burying my face in my hands. "You're relentless, you know that?"

"Thank you," she said sweetly, batting her lashes. "Now, start talking."

I sighed, setting my napkin down as I gathered my thoughts. "Alright, I guess... I could tell you about my family. My parents are... great. Overly invested, maybe, but in a good way."

Caroline grinned. "Define 'overly invested.'"

"They definitely cried when I moved here," I admitted, a rueful smile tugging at my lips. "My mom still calls me every other day to ask if I'm eating enough."

It was a smooth lie, one that rolled off my tongue so naturally it almost felt true. But guilt needled at me anyway, a sharp little pang in my chest. I hadn't spoken to my parents since I'd moved, not because I didn't want to, but because I could already hear the questions: Are you okay? Do you need anything? Why don't you just come back home?

"Aww, that's sweet," Linda said, her voice warm. "It means they love you, you know. My parents were the same—still are, in their own way. At least, my mom is. My dad..." She trailed off, and her smile faltered just slightly before she cleared her throat. "Well, he's as sick as can be these days, but she's there every moment, still trying to put him back together. She always said, 'Love's a full-time job, Linda.' I guess she means it."

The thought had enough emotional power to make me shift in my seat, pushing the guilt down as far as it could go.

"They do," I agreed softly. "But it also makes leaving harder."

"Well, I wouldn't know much about that. I grew up in foster care—parents were more of a myth than a reality." She leaned back, shrugging like it didn't bother her, though the faint edge in her smile said otherwise. "It wasn't all bad, though. I learned to dodge rules like a pro and make spaghetti out of just about anything. I call that a win."

Her grin was sharp and a little too wide, almost daring one of us to press further. Linda didn't, her gaze softening as she reached for her drink.

"You probably make better spaghetti than I do, then," I said lightly, hoping to ease the tension.

"Oh, I doubt that, Ms. Hastings. I'm talking ketchup as a base sauce, a sprinkle of salt, and maybe some hot dogs if it was a good week. A true culinary masterpiece."

The table grew quiet for a beat before Caroline said, "Anyway, is there really no one back home that you left behind? I feel like we all have a questionable love life, but to not have one at all is criminal."

Sam's gaze flickered toward me, his expression unreadable. "You don't have to answer that."

"No, it's okay," I said, surprising even myself. I set my napkin down, my fingers smoothing out the edges as I gathered my thoughts. "There was someone. We were together for a long time—childhood sweethearts, actually."

Caroline leaned forward, her eyebrows lifting, but there was no teasing in her expression this time, just curiosity. "So what happened? You don't have to answer if you don't want to, but childhood sweethearts usually end with happily ever after."

"Well, he cheated on me with my best friend, so."

The words formed so quickly in my head that I almost said them out loud. My fingers curled around the napkin, twisting it until the fabric wrinkled under my vice-like grip. It was the first time I had thought about Derek in weeks— except for his unanswered message, still sitting in my inbox. I glanced down at the napkin, the familiar ache spreading through my chest, but it felt different now. Manageable. Like the dull throb of a bruise that's already fading.

"He cheated on me with my best friend."

Caroline gasped, loud enough to draw the attention of a couple at the next table. She didn't seem to care. "Your best friend?" she said. "What is wrong with people?"

Linda's eyes narrowed like she was mentally sentencing him to life without parole. "That's unforgivable," she muttered, shaking her head.

I forced a small smile, shrugging like it didn't matter anymore. "It was a long time ago," I said, even though "a long time" felt both accurate and like a lie. "And honestly, it just showed me that I was holding on to something that wasn't right for me. We wanted different things—or, I guess, he wanted someone else."

Caroline crossed her arms, her indignation rolling off her in waves. "You're way too calm about this. I hope you at least keyed his car or something."

Linda snorted softly, and her voice took on that dry tone she reserved for Caroline's dramatics. "Caroline, she's a nurse, not an arsonist."

"Yeah, well, maybe I'd have changed careers for him."

That pulled a laugh out of me, and I relaxed a little. "Trust me, he was not worth the effort."

Sam hadn't said a word yet, and when I glanced his way, I found his gaze locked on me. It was steady, almost thoughtful, or like he was trying to piece together a puzzle he didn't want to rush through. "That doesn't make it any less awful," he said quietly.

Caroline shook her head, still fuming. "You're better than me, Imara. I'd have burned his entire life to the ground. And hers."

Linda rolled her eyes. "Caroline, you almost set your curtains on fire the last time you lit a candle."

"Details," Caroline huffed, waving her hand. "I'm just saying—what a jerk."

Linda nodded in agreement. "Caroline's right. You're smart, beautiful, and kind. Some guy out there is going to realize how lucky he is."

I chuckled, shaking my head. "I don't know if I even want that. Not anytime soon, at least. Maybe not at all."

The words tumbled out before I could stop them; the table went silent for a second. Caroline's eyebrows shot up in surprise, and even Sam leaned back slightly, studying me with a curious head tilt.

"Not at all?" Caroline repeated.

I shrugged, my gaze fixed on the condensation sliding down the side of my glass. "I don't know. It's just... not something I'm thinking about right now. Maybe I don't need it to be happy."

Linda smiled knowingly. "There's nothing wrong with that. Happiness looks different for everyone."

Caroline clinked her glass against mine, a conspiratorial grin spreading across her face. "Well, cheers to that."

Sam didn't say much, but his features shifted when I glanced at him. His brow wasn't as furrowed as it usually was when he was thinking through something clinical. Instead, his forehead was smooth, and the faintest lines of concern around his eyes softened into something closer to understanding. His mouth was relaxed, lips parted like he was about to say something, but he changed his mind at the last second.

As the conversation shifted back to lighter topics, I allowed my gaze to drift toward the bar again. The man was gone, but the strange familiarity lingered. It didn't matter, I told myself. It was another passing face in a new town.

The cold, sharp, and bracing night air wrapped around me as we stepped out of the bar. I shivered instinctively and pulled my jacket tighter around myself. Linda and Caroline followed close behind.

"Alright, you've parked on the far end, right?" Linda asked, her tone slipping easily into her motherly role as she zipped up her coat. "Will you be okay?"

I nodded, stuffing my hands into my pockets. "Oh yeah, I'm just over there."

Caroline waved off Linda's concern with a dramatic flourish. "Oh, she'll be fine. Dr. Gallant here is playing escort, aren't you, Sam?" She winked, earning an eye roll from both of us.

"Very funny," Sam replied, his voice dripping with mock seriousness. "But yes, I'll make sure she gets to her car safely. You two go on and get home before Linda starts lecturing us all about frostbite."

Linda snorted but didn't argue. She stepped closer, wrapping me in a brief but tight hug. "If you need anything, just text."

"I'm good," I assured her, my voice soft. "Thanks, Linda. Really."

Caroline casually draped an arm around my shoulders and pulled me in for a quick squeeze. "Don't let him bore you to death with his uh... charm," she joked, pointing a playful finger at Sam before turning and leaving with Linda.

"Text us when you get home!" Linda called over her shoulder as they walked toward their cars, their silhouettes shrinking into the dimly lit parking lot.

Sam gestured toward the parking lot with a nod as the laughter and chatter faded into the background. "Shall we?"

I hesitated for a split second but then fell into step beside him, the crunch of gravel beneath our feet filling the silence. The cold nipped at my nose, and I glanced up at the clear sky; the stars scattered like tiny shards of light. It was peaceful—almost too peaceful after the whirlwind of the bar.

"You didn't have to," I said, breaking the quiet.

"Didn't have to what?" he asked.

"Walk me to my car," I replied, glancing at him. "I'm perfectly capable, you know."

He smirked, shoving his hands into his coat pockets. "I know you are. But how would it look having you walking in this scary empty parking lot alone?

"Like a man who values a woman's independence?" I shot back, side-eyeing him as I tightened my scarf against the wind. "But what do I know?"

We both chuckled, and my breath puffed out in front of me, visible in the frigid air. I shoved my hands deeper into my coat pockets. I was just about to thank him for walking me when he spoke again.

"You know," he started, "What you said earlier about not wanting anyone..."

I tensed slightly, glancing at him from the corner of my eye. "Yeah?"

He slowed just a little and looked down at the ground as if he were choosing his words carefully. "I get it. After someone has hurt you deeply, it's hard to imagine opening yourself up again. But keeping your heart closed off doesn't protect you as much as you think it does. Heartbreak is part of life. It means you cared. It means you tried."

When I didn't reply, he continued, his tone a little lighter now. "Just... keep it open. You never know what—or who— might surprise you."

I glanced at him, and for the briefest moment, his warm and steady eyes met mine. Something in them made my stomach flip in a way I was not entirely comfortable with.

I forced a laugh, hoping to deflect. "You sound like one of those cheesy inspirational posters."

Sam chuckled, the sound low and rich. "Maybe. But that doesn't mean I'm wrong."

We reached my car, and I turned to him, hoping to steer the conversation into safer territory. "Thanks for walking me. I think I can take it from here."

"Anytime," he said, leaning back slightly as if giving me space. But before I could open the door, he added, almost as an afterthought, "You deserve good things, Imara. Just... don't forget that."

I forced a tight and polite smile and nodded before slipping into the driver's seat. The door shut with a soft thud, but his words hung in the air, stubbornly refusing to leave with him. As I started the car, I watched him walk away through the windshield, his shoulders slightly hunched against the cold.

I gripped the steering wheel a tad too tightly as his voice replayed in my mind like a broken record. "You deserve good things."

I was not stupid. I could see what this was: it was Dr. Whitak seeing me in ways I wish he wouldn't. It would be so easy to let someone like him in. Too easy.

He was everything Derek wasn't. Calm, patient, a fixer. The kind of man who could anchor you when you felt adrift. But that's the thing about anchors—they hold you down. Right now, I didn't want anything—besides myself—to hold me down.

The thought of opening myself up again, of peeling back the layers I've so carefully rebuilt, felt like pressing on a fresh bruise. Suffocating. Risking another heartbreak wasn't something I could give right now, not to Sam or anyone else.

I released a shaky breath, flipped on the heat, and focused on the frost melting from the windshield. The sooner I stopped thinking about this, the better I'd be, or so I told myself.

CHAPTER 17: SAFE SPACE

"Imara Hastings."

Linda had tucked her hair neatly behind her ears. "What are you sneaking around for, huh? You look like you're avoiding the cafeteria cops."

I tried for an innocent smile. "Me? Sneaking? Never. Just... expertly navigating."

Linda snorted. "Uh-huh. Expertly navigating my radar, more like."

"I'd never try to avoid your radar, Linda. I promise."

Linda sighed, shaking her head as she leaned against the counter. Her lips curved into a faint smile that I could only describe as an equal mix of fondness and exasperation.

"You bring a different air to this place, Imara. And you," she added, pointing her mug at me like a gavel, "are the best hire we've had in years. You're making the rest of us look bad."

I rolled my eyes playfully as I grabbed a fresh cup for myself. "I'll take that as a compliment. Even though I'm pretty sure you just want me to cover your weekend shift."

"You caught me," she said, feigning innocence. "But seriously, you're doing great. I wish you'd stay here forever. Vermont agrees with you."

The unexpected sincerity in her voice made me pause. "Thanks, Linda. That really means a lot."

"Don't get all mushy on me now," she said, smirking. "You'll make me cry, and then I'll have to ruin my tough-love reputation."

I laughed as I sipped my coffee. "I'll try not to tarnish your legacy."

"Good. Now get out of here before I change my mind and assign you double rounds."

Shaking my head with a smile, I headed toward my locker. My phone buzzed just as I was slipping on my coat. It was Charlotte.

I swiped to answer. "Imara Hastings," I said, a little mock-formal.

"How does my mysterious foreign friend feel about wine on a weeknight?"

I couldn't help but smile at how playful she'd said "foreign," like I was some exotic novelty instead of just a woman from a few states away.

I rolled my eyes, leaning against the lockers. "Foreign? You know I'm just a few states away, right? Not a different continent."

"Please," she snorted. "Anyone who survives these winters without being born into them is basically an alien."

The sound that left my mouth wasn't a far cry between a strangled animal and a hyena. I looked around quickly, covering my mouth to ensure another one didn't escape.

"Well, I'm still on shift right now, and wine sounds like a dangerous proposition."

"Dangerous, sure," she replied. "But therapeutic. Come on, I'm sure you've worked hard all week poking needles and handling blood. I'll even promise not to pry too much."

I laughed softly. "Alright, Charlotte. What time?"

"Eight. Don't be late, and don't bring your city boots—they'll freeze to the driveway before you get to my door."

"Oh, I'm absolutely wearing them now. Someone's gotta show the snow who's boss."

"Fine, but don't come crying to me when you're stuck halfway up the driveway, doing the penguin shuffle."

When the call ended, it left a faint smile on my face as I tucked my phone away.

The drive to Charlotte's house was quiet. The snowbanks piled high along the road glew faintly under the streetlights.

When I pulled into her driveway, her house came into view, and I couldn't help but smile. It was simple but warm, with dark green shutters and a cozy little porch with fairy lights strung from it. It suited her perfectly: it was charming without trying too hard and inviting without being flashy.

Charlotte met me at the door, her signature pixie cut slightly tousled and a glass of wine already in hand. "Welcome to my humble abode," she said, stepping aside to let me in. The warmth from inside greeted me instantly, along with the faint scent of sandalwood and something citrusy.

Her living room was like stepping into a Pinterest board brought to life—cozy without feeling cluttered, with shelves lined with books, crystals, and tiny potted plants. A woven rug with intricate patterns stretched across the floor and a cluster of mismatched lamps in the corner gave off a soft glow.

"This place…" I trailed off, shaking my head in amazement. "It's like a sanctuary."

Charlotte chuckled, shutting the door behind me. "That's the goal. Life's chaotic enough; home should be the opposite."

She led me to the couch, already set with a small tray of cheese, crackers, and grapes. "Wine or red wine?" she asked, holding up two bottles with a mischievous grin.

"Red," I said, settling into the plush cushions. "But just one glass—I've got work in the morning."

"Responsible," she said with a mock frown as she poured the wine and handed me a glass. She dropped into the armchair across me, crossed her legs, and tucked one foot underneath her. "Alright, let's get to the real question. Are you settling into Vermont life or already mapping out an escape plan?"

I chuckled, swirling the wine in my glass. "Somewhere in between, honestly."

She laughed, tilting her head. "I knew it. Vermont has that effect—it's either love at first snowfall or a slow descent into 'what have I done?'"

I couldn't help but relax as we fell into an easy conversation. As it inevitably does, it was not long before the topic shifted to relationships—or, in her case, the lack thereof.

"I've been happily single for... what, eight years now?" she said, leaning back in her chair. "And I don't mean 'happily single' in the 'I'm waiting for the right person to come along' kind of way. I mean it. I love my life exactly the way it is."

Her confidence was captivating. "You've never wanted to—?"

"Settle down? Have kids? The white picket fence?" she finished, her tone wry. "Nope. Not once. Don't get me wrong—I love love. I think it's beautiful. But it's not for me."

I blinked, caught off guard by her certainty. "How did you figure that out?"

Charlotte shrugged, her gaze thoughtful. "It wasn't some grand epiphany. It was little things. Every time I tried to fit myself into the mold everyone expected, I felt... wrong. Like I was living someone else's life. It took a while, but I realized I didn't need to follow anyone else's script to be happy."

Her words settled over me like a warm blanket and made me question everything I'd ever believed about what life was 'supposed' to look like. "That's... brave," I said quietly. "I don't think I've ever thought about it like that."

"Brave? Nah," Charlotte said, waving me off. "The world would be a lot easier if more of us admitted what we really wanted instead of chasing what we think we should want."

I took another sip of my drink, her words echoing in my mind.

What do I really want? The question felt impossibly large.

I swirled the wine in my glass, watching the tiny bubbles rise to the surface. Charlotte's words still hovered in the air, heavy with truth, and I felt a lump forming in my throat. What did I really want? I'd been so consumed by what I'd lost and by what I thought I needed that I hadn't dared to ask myself that question.

Charlotte leaned back in her chair, her sharp, discerning gaze softening as she watched me. "You're quiet again. Does that mean something's brewing in there?" she said, tapping her temple with a knowing smirk.

I chuckled lightly, the sound almost foreign to my own ears. "It's just... I've been thinking a lot about what I'm supposed to want. Or what I thought I wanted. And how maybe none of it was ever really about me."

Her expression didn't change, but I could tell she was listening intently and giving me the space to speak if I wanted to. And before I could second-guess myself, the words came tumbling out.

"I was with someone for years," I began, my voice steady despite the ache that twists in my chest. "We grew up together. Everyone thought we were perfect for each other. And I believed it, too. Or maybe I just convinced myself I did."

Charlotte nodded, her face free of pity or judgment, just a quiet understanding that urged me on.

"But then," I continued, my fingers tightening around the glass, "I found out he was cheating with my best friend."

The words hung in the air, heavier than I anticipated, and for a moment, I felt the sting of them all over again. "I thought... I thought we were building something real and working toward something: marriage, a family, a life together, all of it. And now... now I don't even know if I want any of that anymore."

Charlotte didn't flinch nor say anything right away. Instead, she leaned forward slightly, her elbows resting on her knees. "That's a hell of a betrayal," she said softly. "And I'm not gonna feed you some nonsense about how you'll be stronger for it. But I will say this—you get to decide what comes next. Not them. Not anyone else."

I felt my shoulders relax, and tension I hadn't realized I was carrying hauling started ebbing away. I take another sip of my wine.

A crooked photo caught my eye. It was Charlotte, younger but unmistakable, standing in a sunflower field with a group of kids who all shared the same too-wide grin.

After a moment, Charlotte said, "Do you know the funny thing about heartbreak? It doesn't just tear you apart. It cracks you open. It's messy and awful, but sometimes... sometimes, it makes room for something better."

"It doesn't feel like there's room for anything right now,"

Charlotte carefully and deliberately set her glass down on the coffee table. "That's okay," she said softly, leaning forward. "It doesn't have to. Not yet. You don't have to rush healing. It comes when it comes."

When she got up to refill her glass, I leaned back against the couch and let out a shaky breath.

By the time the evening wound down, Charlotte stretched her arms over her head, looking at me with a grin that I considered way too sincere for my liking. "You're gonna be okay, Imara," she said, pulling me into a hug that I definitely wasn't ready for. Her arms wrapped around me like a warm cocoon, and before I could think of a snarky remark, she added, "And you're not alone. Not here."

Her arms wrapped around me like a warm cocoon, and for a split second, I froze.

Are all Vermonters this accepting, warm, and fuzzy? Was this hugging strangers into submission a thing they taught in school up here? Still, I melted into it, slowly, awkwardly, like a popsicle left out in the sun. I was not completely comfortable, but I was glad that I was not navigating this new life entirely alone.

When I stepped outside into the chilly night air, I glanced back at her house, its warm glow spilling onto the snow-covered lawn, and something stirred inside me. Maybe this is what it meant to start over—not just running from the past but letting new connections and possibilities take root.

As I drove home, I didn't feel quite as untethered. For the first time in a long time, I felt... grounded.

CHAPTER 18: PRACTICALLY UNSTOPPABLE

I woke up to the sound of a plow scraping the street outside, and for a split second, I felt disoriented. When I rolled out of bed, I caught sight of myself in the mirror.

My hair was doing the absolute most.

I grabbed a pair of scissors that were definitely not designed for haircuts (don't judge me) and shuffled to the bathroom. The fluorescent light flickered once as if it was already judging my life choices, but I ignored it. After a splash of warm water and a generous glob of coconut oil to bribe the rebellion into submission, I assessed the situation in the mirror.

"Just a trim," I told my reflection. "No need to get carried away."

The first snip felt both terrifying and liberating. The second snip was... questionable. But by the third, I'd convinced myself I missed my calling as a professional stylist. I applied gel to the edges, smoothing everything into place, and stepped back. The mirror revealed... well, not perfection, but something close enough. The short curls still had a mind of their own, but I shrugged, deciding to call it character.

To seal the deal, I reached for my favorite gold hoops—the ones that had magical powers to make me look more put together than I actually was—and clasp them in with a satisfied nod. "Look at you," I said, grinning at my reflection. "Practically unstoppable."

The smell of buttered toast filled my small kitchen as I spread a generous layer of jam across the crispy surface, the knife clinking lightly against the plate. I was halfway to taking a bite when my phone buzzed on the counter.

I glanced at the screen. Dr. Whitaker.

My first thought was: Why is he calling me on a Sunday? My second thought was: It better not be about work.

Sighing, I wiped my hands on a dish towel and grabbed the phone. As much as I wanted to ignore it, a tiny voice at the back of my head whispered: What if it's serious?

"Hello?" I answered, trying not to sound as annoyed as I felt.

"Dr. Whitaker," I said, trying to inject just the right amount of playful irritation into my tone. "If this is about work, I'll have you know my schedule is sacred on weekends. That's when I hydrate, moisturize, and mind my business."

There was a brief pause before he responded, his voice laced with just enough amusement to keep me from hanging up. "Good morning to you, too, Imara. And no, it's not about work. Not... exactly."

I sighed, my fingers drumming lightly on the counter. "You really have a way with clarity, you know that?"

"It's a health fair," he said, skipping right over my sarcasm. "In Northfield. We're short a few hands, and I thought you might want to help out. After all, it's part of the program, and I figured... well, you might like this one. But no pressure."

I let his words hang in the air for a second as I crossed the kitchen to grab my plate. "Hmm. On one hand, I had planned a rigorous day of couch therapy. On the other, I did say I'd stay involved."

"Such selflessness," he quipped, and I could almost hear the grin in his voice. "Truly inspiring."

I glanced at my reflection in the microwave door, rolling my eyes as I adjusted my hair. "You're lucky I'm a woman of my word, Dr. Whitaker.

"I'll be right there in the trenches with you. This one's a little different—more hands-on health education. We've got screenings, some wellness demos, and a mini-clinic setup. It's a good one."

The truth is, I was not sure I should. Spending more time with Dr. Whitaker, especially after what he said the last time he walked me to my car, felt complicated.

"Fine," I said, dragging the word out like it cost me something. "But only because you've caught me in a moment of weakness."

"That's the spirit," he replied, and I swear I could hear the grin stretching across his face. "I'll pick you up in an hour."

"Wait, what? No one said anything about door-to-door service."

"See you soon, Imara."

After we hung up, I set my phone down and glanced around the apartment. I would say that he was interrupting my serenity. It was quiet and peaceful. But I knew the stillness would start creeping under my skin if I stayed here too long.

Yet, spending time with him felt like stepping onto thin ice. His words from the other night replayed in my head, soft and lingering: You deserve good things.

I shook off the thought, forcing myself to move. "Alright, Hastings," I muttered as I made my way to the bedroom to grab a jacket. "An hour. You can survive an hour."

Outside, the air was sharp enough to sting my cheeks as I stepped out, clutching my coat closed with one hand while locking the door with the other. My breath, little puffs that disappeared almost as quickly as they formed, clouded the air in front of me.

Sam's car sat at the curb, the engine humming softly, and I could just make out his silhouette through the frosted window.

As I approached, the driver's side window rolled down, and he leaned out slightly, one hand on the steering wheel, the other raised in a casual wave.

"Morning!" he called out, his grin wide and warm enough to rival the car heater.

"Morning," I replied, my voice muffled by the scarf I was adjusting. He didn't move to open the door for me, which I was grateful for—it was one less thing to overthink. Instead, I pulled it open myself and slid into the passenger seat. Immediately, a mix of pine air freshener and something faintly antiseptic, like the ghosts of hand sanitizer past, hit me.

A stack of patient files was neatly buckled into the backseat; a reusable coffee cup sat in the holder, and a crumpled receipt on the console that I could just make out read "café au lait." The seat warmer was already on, and I sighed as the heat seeped through my coat.

Sam's gray sweater fit comfortably over broad shoulders, his hair slightly mussed like he'd been up for hours but couldn't be bothered to fix it. He glanced over at me with a smile that was far too chipper for this early in the day, holding out a steaming cup of coffee. "For you."

I took it, my hands wrapping around the warmth automatically. "Thanks," I mumbled, lifting it to my lips. He twisted around, reaching into the back. I heard the rustle of a bag before he turned back to me, holding out a small box of chocolates neatly tied with a ribbon and a single red rose. He gently placed them in my lap, his grin widening like he'd just done the most casual thing in the world.

"Figured you might need a little extra pick-me-up today," he said.

"Oh... that's thoughtful, but I—"

"Don't even think about it," he cut in, his voice teasing but firm. "Just take them. Everyone deserves a little something nice."

"I don't really eat chocolate," I managed, my voice faltering as I glanced up at him. He didn't seem fazed; instead, he waved a hand like I'd just told him it might rain later.

"Consider it an experiment," he said. "You never know—it might grow on you."

I mustered another thank you, but my stomach churned as I adjusted the box and rose on my lap. The coffee I was just savoring felt too hot now.

I glanced at the rose again, its red petals somehow more glaring in the small space of the car. Was this thoughtful?

"Don't be a naive idiot, Imara," I thought. Sam didn't seem to notice my internal spiral as he shifted the car into gear.

"Ready for another health fair adventure?"

I exhaled slowly, my fingers brushing over the ribbon on the chocolate box as I sat up straighter in my seat. "Yup," I said, adjusting the rose so it was not poking at my arm. My voice came out a little too bright for my liking, so I cleared my throat and nodded firmly as if trying to convince myself. "Let's do this."

The car glided down the frost-lined streets, the crunch of tires against the icy pavement filling the silence between us. Vermont looked like a postcard: snow-dusted evergreens, icicles hanging from roof edges, and the occasional puff of smoke rising from chimneys. I tried to focus on the scenery, letting it distract me from the small red rose that seemed to burn a hole through my lap.

Sam chatted about the event, listing off volunteers and the planned activities, but his words blurred as I stole glances at him. He was relaxed, one hand on the steering wheel, the other drumming lightly against his thigh in rhythm with the song playing softly on the radio. It was an easy confidence that made him so... Sam.

I shook my head slightly and turned my attention back to the window. This was going to be a long day.

The parking lot was abuzz, with volunteers unloading boxes of supplies, families bundled in layers against the cold, and a few kids darting between booths with the kind of energy that made me miss being that age. Sam pulled into a spot near the entrance and glanced over at me with a grin.

"Let's get to work," he said, popping the trunk.

I hopped out, grateful for the blast of cold air that cleared my thoughts. The rose and chocolate were safe in the car, but their memory lingered. I followed Sam to the back, where he was already grabbing a box marked "First Aid Kits" and balancing it on one arm.

"You good with this one?" he asked, holding out a smaller box labeled PPE.

"Yeah, I've got it," I replied, hefting it up. I stepped aside just in time to avoid being run over by another volunteer wheeling in a dolly stacked with boxes labeled Vaccine Supplies.

The tables had a draped-over layer of colorful banners that flapped lightly in the breeze, and the volunteers were already bustling to set up stations for free check-ups, vaccinations, and health education. The scent of powdered donuts mingled with the crisp tang of alcohol wipes, and I caught a brief glimpse of a tray stacked with individual fruit cups near the registration table.

Sam gestured toward the center of the room. "I'll be floating around if you need me."

"Got it," I said, already scanning for familiar faces. I spotted a few volunteers I remembered from the last event: Darlene, with gray curls peeking out from under a knit hat as she ran the registration table, and Andy.

"Imara!" Darlene called out, her smile bright as she waved me over. "Glad to see you again!"

"Same here," I said, setting my box down on her table. "Where do you need me?"

"You're a gem," she said, tapping her clipboard. " "Flu shots—booth three. The nurse there could use an extra set of hands."

I dove in, helping organize the flow of people, chatting with a few patients, and occasionally trading jokes with Andy when our paths crossed.

Sam was everywhere, somehow managing to be in ten places at once. He checked in with volunteers, chatted with patients, and even kneeled to tie the loose boot of a kid who couldn't have been more than five. The kid grinned, pointing at something behind him, and Sam actually stopped to listen, thinking that whatever this tiny human was saying was the most important thing in the world.

It was endearing, I guess. I hate to admit it, but it was. The way he moved, effortlessly weaving through the chaos with this unshakable sense of purpose, made it seem like he was born to thrive in all this noise. It was impressive. Objectively. But then there was the way his gaze lingered when it landed on me. Not often, but just enough to make me wonder if it was all in my head.

And I hated the confusion it stirred. Logic told me I should like him. He was kind, steady, the complete opposite of Derek in every way that matters. But my heart wasn't even close to being in it. Not with him. Not with anyone. My brain jumped into the motion, screaming that I was not ready and had barely started rebuilding myself.

"Imara, are you with us?" Darlene teased, snapping me out of my thoughts. "Too busy watching your favorite doctor?"

My head snapped up so fast that I nearly dropped the clipboard. "What? No!" The words burst out of me louder than I intended, and I cleared my throat quickly, forcing a light laugh.

"I mean, come on, Darlene. That's not—no."

Darlene hummed, her knowing look not budging an inch. "Sure, sure. For what it's worth, though, he's a good one. Kind, hardworking... not bad on the eyes, either."

"Darlene," I warned, my tone firm but laced with humor. "Are you trying to start rumors now?"

She smirked, nudging me with her elbow. "Rumors? Please. I'm just saying, if he happens to like you, you could do worse."

I rolled my eyes, biting back the smile threatening to break through. "Let's focus on getting these patients sorted, shall we? That's why we're here, isn't it?"

"Whatever you say, Nurse Hastings," she said with a laugh, turning back to the line forming at her station. "But don't think I'm letting this go."

I shook my head, biting back a smile as I refocused on the clipboard in my hands. The last thing I needed was someone here who thought there was something between Sam and me. Between registering patients, assisting with screenings, and distributing supplies, I barely had time to think.

By the time the fair started winding down, I was exhausted but oddly content. As I packed up my station, I glanced across the room and caught sight of Sam. He was deep in conversation with one of the coordinators, his hands moving animatedly as he talked. But then his gaze flickered to me, and he quirked a brow—almost like he was asking, How are you holding up?

I nodded in response, and he turned back to the conversation. "What am I supposed to do with you, Dr. Whitaker?"

CHAPTER 19: POSTCARDS

A sharp knock startled me as I hung my coat up on my rack near the front door. I spun toward the door, half expecting it to be Charlotte or someone from work. Instead, I opened it to find my ever-pleasant neighbor, Mr. Thompson, standing there, a brown envelope in hand.

"This yours?" He grumbled, his eyebrows knit together in what I'd come to recognize as his default expression. "It was in my mailbox."

"Hey, Mr. Thompson. It seems that it is, thanks," I said, taking it from him carefully. His presence always felt like it was teetering on the edge of a lecture, and I braced myself for whatever he might say next.

"Keep an eye on your mail," he muttered. "Don't need the post office thinking I've got two houses to deal with."

"I'll do that," I replied, holding back a smile. "Thanks for bringing it over."

He grunted in acknowledgment and turned to leave without another word. I closed the door behind him, shaking my head as I headed to the couch.

I sat on the couch, the envelope sliding off my lap and landing on the cushion beside me as the postcard caught my eye. Bright colors, bent corners. The kind of card you picked up on a whim, not because it was special, but because it felt like a small way to say I'm thinking of you.

I reached for it slowly, my movements deliberate, like touching it too fast might break something fragile. My thumb brushed the edge as I flipped it over. The scrawl of my mom's handwriting greeted me, looping and slightly tilted, like always. I read the words once or twice before they started to sink in.

Hope Vermont isn't freezing you out, sweetheart. Don't forget to eat something warm, wear a hat, and call us. Love you to pieces, Mom.

A tiny heart punctuated her note, the same one she'd used to sign everything since I was a kid—birthday cards, permission slips, even grocery lists stuck to the fridge. It was so her. It was so her... and it knocked the breath out of me.

My dad's note was shorter, like always.

We miss you, kiddo. Take care of yourself. -Dad.

I traced the ink with my thumb, feeling the indentations of their pens, the physical proof that they sat down and wrote this together. It was such a small thing, a postcard, but the weight of it in my hand felt like miles collapsing, like all the distance I put between us pressing down at once.

I hadn't realized how far I'd pushed them to the back of my mind. It was easier that way. Easier to focus on the move, the new job, and the unfamiliar faces in this unfamiliar place. It was easier not to think about the hurt in their voices when I told them I was leaving. But this little card dragged it all to the surface.

The ache was sudden and sharp. Not just guilt, though that was there too. It was everything: missing Sunday dinners, my mom's laugh echoing through the kitchen, the way my dad would just sit with me in silence when the world felt too loud. Here I was, holding a piece of them in my hands, feeling like a stranger to my own family.

I pressed the card against my chest, the edges crinkling under my grip. My throat tightened, and I blinked quickly, willing the tears to stay where they were because crying over a postcard felt ridiculous.

The phone on the table caught my eye; its screen was dark but somehow glaring. Calling them felt monumental, like opening a door I'd spent months keeping locked. But as I sat there, staring at the postcard and the phone, I realized I no longer had a choice.

My fingers hovered over my mom's name in my contacts. My chest felt tight, my breath shallow. I didn't know what I'd say or if I'd even say anything that made sense. But I owed them this.

I pressed the button, bringing the phone to my ear, the postcard still clutched tightly in my other hand. The line rang once, twice, and then her voice.

"Imara?"

"Hi, Mom."

"Oh my God," she breathed, her words tumbling out in a rush. "I—your father and I were just talking about you. We were worried, sweetheart. You haven't called, not even a text. I didn't know if I had to ask the hospital for your address." Her voice cracked, and my throat tightened painfully.

"I know," I said, guilt settling heavy in my chest. "I'm sorry, Mom. I should've called sooner. I just..." I glance around my quiet apartment, suddenly wishing the walls weren't so bare. "I didn't know what to say."

"You don't have to say anything," she replied quickly, and I could picture her standing in the kitchen, the phone clutched tightly in her hand. "We just wanted to know you were okay."

"I'm okay," I said, though the words feel insufficient. "I'm... adjusting. Work keeps me busy."

There was a shuffle on her end, and then my dad's voice came through. "Imara. Kiddo, it's good to hear your voice."

Hearing him made something in me crack. I pressed my free hand to my forehead as I fought to keep my emotions in check. "Hi, Dad."

"You had your mom worried sick," he said. "You know how she gets."

"I know," I whispered, ashamed. "I didn't mean to worry you guys. I just needed some time."

"We figured as much," he said. "That's why we didn't push. But you've got to give us something, Imara. A call, a text, even just to say you're alive."

"I will," I promised. "I'm sorry. Really."

My mom's voice broke in again, softer this time. "We sent you a postcard. Did you get it?"

"I did," I admitted, bringing my arm up to look at the postcard still clutched tightly in my hand. "It was nice. Thank you."

"You're eating, right?" she asked. "And dressing warm? I saw on the news it's been freezing up there."

"I'm fine, Mom," I said, trying to inject some reassurance into my tone. "I'm eating, and I've got plenty of layers. I promise."

"We just miss you, sweetheart," she said quietly. "That's all."

The lump in my throat swelled again, louder this time, but I swallowed hard, forcing myself to respond. "I miss you too. I'll call more often. I promise."

The silence that followed felt full, almost fragile, but it didn't last long. My dad cleared his throat, breaking the moment. "Good. That's all we ask. Now, tell us about this new job of yours."

They asked about Vermont, the hospital, and whether I'd met anyone interesting. I kept my answers light, telling them about Linda, Caroline, Charlotte, and only some of Sam.

When the call finally ended, I sat there for a brief 'check-in' moment, staring at the postcard on the table. It felt different now—less like a reminder of what I'd avoided and more like a lifeline.

I let myself wonder if real, lasting fulfillment could come from somewhere other than the places I'd always looked. Maybe it didn't have to be tied to a romantic partner or the idea of building a life with someone else. Maybe it didn't have to mean returning to the life I left behind, either.

CHAPTER 20: LAVENDER

My phone buzzed loudly against the nightstand, dragging me out of sleep. I squinted at the screen, the harsh glow making my eyes water.

"Charlotte," I groaned, hitting the answer button with a groggy swipe. "It's five in the morning. Someone better be dying."

"Imara," Charlotte chirped, far too awake for this hour. "Get your butt up. We're going to the farmer's market."

I blinked at the ceiling, trying to process. "I have a shift today. You know, that thing where I save lives for a living?"

"You don't start until eight. That's plenty of time," she countered, unbothered. "I'll be outside in ten minutes. Wear something you don't mind getting dirty."

"Dirty?" I echoed, but the line went dead. Of course.

I dragged myself out of bed, muttering under my breath about overly cheerful morning people. After throwing on a sweatshirt and jeans, I smoothed over my hair and stumbled into the kitchen to grab a quick breakfast.

By the time Charlotte's car pulled up, I was more awake but no less confused about why we were doing this.

Charlotte inhaled deeply, holding out her arms wide. "Isn't this the best way to start a morning?"

I eyed her, stuffing myself into the passenger side. "Debatable."

She laughed, the sound way too cheerful for this hour. "You'll thank me later. Farmer's markets are like therapy but with better snacks."

I muttered something unintelligible as I buckled my seatbelt, squinting against the sunrise and spilling through the windshield. Charlotte hummed along to the radio as we drove, clearly in her element.

The market was already alive by the time we pulled into the crowded lot. People milled about with woven baskets and canvas totes, their chatter blending with the occasional bark of a dog or the rustle of leaves in the crisp morning breeze.

Charlotte parked with alarming precision, practically leaping out of the car. "Come on, Imara," she called over her shoulder. "This is going to be great."

I followed her, less leaping, more dragging my feet. The air smelled of fresh bread, earthy produce, and something sugary I couldn't quite place. My stomach rumbled, reminding me I only had toast earlier.

Charlotte grabbed my hand and tugged me toward a stall overflowing with apples in every shade of red and green imaginable. "Look at these! Don't they just scream autumn?"

"They scream pie," I muttered, picking up a glossy red one.

"Morning, Henry," Charlotte called to an older man arranging baskets of apples. "Got any of those Honeycrisps left?"

"For you, Charlotte? Always." Henry winked, pulling a small bag of apples from behind the stall and handing it to her. "These are the best of the batch."

Charlotte tossed an apple my way, and I caught it with all the grace of someone trying to juggle fire. The apple bounced off my hand and into the crook of my arm. Thankfully, I managed to recover it just before it hit the ground, holding it up triumphantly like I meant to do all that.

"You wouldn't survive on a farm, Imara— maybe as one of the tasters. But go on, try it. They're good," she said, nudging me. "Trust me."

I rolled my eyes but took a bite anyway, the crunch oddly satisfying.

As we strolled through the market, Charlotte paused at every other stall like she was running for mayor. She picked up a soft gray one at a table piled high with knitted scarves, then wrapped it around her neck as she chatted with the vendor. I watched as she complimented the intricate patterns, her voice warm and effortless like she'd known the woman for years.

I lingered a few steps behind, my fingers brushing over jars of local honey on display. The glass was cool under my touch, and the golden liquid inside glowed under the soft morning sunlight.

I caught myself mirroring her energy—offering genuine smiles, making small talk about the weather, and even asking about the best ways to store produce. It was subtle, but I felt it: the walls I'd built were slowly loosening their hold.

"Imara, you have to try this," Charlotte said, pulling me from my thoughts. She handed me a slice of bread smeared with something creamy and green.

I squinted at it skeptically. "What is it? Avocado toast's Vermont cousin?"

"Close. Maple-infused goat cheese with chives. Trust me, it's life-changing."

I stared at her, then at the bread, before taking a cautious bite. To my surprise, it was not bad. The cheese was tangy but mellowed by the subtle sweetness of maple, and the bread was perfectly crusty.

I nodded slowly. "Okay, that's... unexpectedly delicious."

Charlotte grinned, clapping her hands together like I'd just validated her entire existence. "Told you! The locals know their stuff."

We continued down the rows, pausing every now and then for Charlotte to chat up vendors like old friends. Meanwhile, I was learning how easy it is to lose track of time in a place like this—where the air smells of fresh bread and cider, and the world seems to shrink to just this: a community coming alive.

"You know," Charlotte said as we paused by a stall selling handmade jewelry, "you're settling in better than you think. I see the way Linda and Caroline look at you. You've already got a little Vermont crew."

I glanced at her, sheepish but unable to hold back a small smile. "Yeah, maybe I do," I admitted, my voice quieter than I'd intended. "It's nice, actually. They've made it easier."

"Of course they have," Charlotte said, her tone matter-of-fact. "You're impossible not to like, Imara. Everyone thinks so, and that's really saying something. We're accustomed to being polite– but from a distance."

I laughed, shaking my head as I picked up a delicate bracelet with tiny maple leaf charms. "Let's not get carried away."

Charlotte smirked, crossing her arms. "I'm just saying— you're not as much of an outsider as you think. Vermont suits you."

For the first time, I let myself believe it might be true.

Charlotte shook her head, her pixie cut catching the light as she turned. "And you know, belonging doesn't happen overnight. It's like a plant. You have to give it time to grow roots. And you, my dear, are putting down some solid ones."

Charlotte paused at a flower stall, her gaze flitting over the array of colorful bouquets. She picked up one—a mix of daisies, wildflowers, and sprigs of lavender—and held it out to me with a warm smile.

"Here," she said. "You're blooming."

I laughed, shaking my head as I took the bouquet. "That's a little on the nose, don't you think?"

"Maybe," she said, her grin unwavering. "But it's true. I've seen it."

I glanced down at the flowers, the soft petals brushing against my fingers. As we started walking again, weaving through the bustling market, I found myself hesitating.

"Can I ask you something?"

Charlotte slowed her pace, her brow slightly furrowing as she turned to me. "Of course," she said, her tone softening, the playful edge she carried just moments ago melting away. She adjusted her tote bag over her shoulder, her full attention now on me. "What's on your mind?"

I took a deep breath, fiddling with the ribbon tied around the bouquet. "Let's say... you have this colleague. They're great—kind, helpful, genuinely good at what they do—but sometimes, I don't know, they cross lines that make you uncomfortable. Not intentionally, I don't think, but still."

Charlotte's frown was immediate. "What kind of lines?"

"I don't know," I said quickly, my words tumbling out in a rush. "It's not anything overt. Just little things. Like too many compliments or gestures that feel a bit too personal. And it's not all the time. Most of the time, they're fine."

Charlotte stopped walking and turned to face me fully. "Imara, if it's making you uncomfortable, it doesn't matter how small it seems. You have every right to feel how you feel."

I nodded, but my chest felt tight. "It's just... they're not doing it intentionally, you know? I think they're just trying to be nice. And I don't want to ruin a good working relationship over something that might just be in my head."

Charlotte narrowed her eyes, her voice firm. "Kindness doesn't give anyone a free pass to overstep boundaries. Have you told them how you feel?"

"No," I admitted, the word heavy in my throat.

"Then that's your first step," she said. "You don't have to make it a big deal, but you need to let them know where the line is. And if they're as good as you say, they'll respect that."

I hesitated, the thought of having that conversation making my stomach churn. "What if they don't?"

"Then you take it further," Charlotte said without missing a beat. "Go to HR and report it. You shouldn't have to feel uncomfortable at work, Imara. Period."

"No," I said quickly, shaking my head. "It's not... it's not like that. I don't think it's anything reportable."

Charlotte studied me for a long moment. "Promise me you won't just brush it under the rug. You deserve to feel safe and respected, no matter how good they are at their job."

I nodded, clutching the bouquet a little tighter. "I'll think about it."

"Good." Charlotte looped her arm through mine as we started walking again, her tone lighter now. "And if you need backup, you know where to find me. I'll personally storm the hospital and set them straight."

Linda and Caroline caught up with me near the nurse's station, both mid-laugh about something undoubtedly ridiculous.

"Did you see that guy in 3B?" Caroline said, gesturing dramatically. "He tried to convince me his blood pressure spikes were because of my 'intimidating energy.'"

Linda raised an eyebrow, her lips twitching. "That sounds suspiciously like something you would say."

Caroline gasped, clutching her chest as if she'd borne a mortal wound. "Linda! Are you accusing me of projecting? I'm offended. Deeply."

"Offended or not, I'm not wrong," Linda retorted, smirking as she crossed her arms. "Intimidating energy, my foot. You probably talked the poor man's pressure through the roof."

I tried to bite back a grin but failed. "To be fair, she does have a way of making people's heads spin."

"Et tu, Imara?" Caroline groaned, throwing her hands up. "You're supposed to be on my side!"

"Sorry," I said, shrugging innocently. "Can't argue with the evidence."

We were just turning the corner toward the breakroom when I nearly collided with someone. I stepped back quickly, muttering a quick "Sorry" before realizing who it was.

Sam.

"Morning, Imara," he said, holding up a familiar box of chocolates and the single red rose I'd left in his car yesterday. "You forgot these."

My stomach plummeted, and I could feel the heat rising to my cheeks. "Oh—thanks," I stammered, reaching out to grab them.

Linda and Caroline's eyes darted between us like hawks spotting prey, and I could practically hear the gears turning in their heads. Before they could say anything, I forced a laugh and added, "Totally slipped my mind. Thanks for dropping them off."

Sam's brow furrowed slightly. "You left them in my car. I thought you might—"

"Right," I cut him off, clutching the items to my chest like they might explode. "You're very... thoughtful. Thanks."

I didn't give him a chance to finish whatever he was about to say. With a quick, "Gotta do my rounds!" I darted past him, ignoring the amused looks from Linda and Caroline as I disappeared down the hallway.

Once inside my office, I closed the door behind me and leaned against it, my heart pounding. The chocolates and rose felt heavier than they should have, and my mind raced with ways to explain them if anyone asked. Not that anyone would ask, but you never know.

He'd been sweet, considerate, and—let's not sugarcoat it— gorgeous. Those sharp cheekbones, that warm, effortless smile, the way he listened, and the fact that he could easily make anyone feel like they were the only person in the room. It would be so easy to fall for someone like him.

But it didn't feel right.

I rubbed my temples, willing the knot in my chest to loosen. It was not just the timing, even though that was a big part of it. It was everything. It was the fact that I still felt like I was piecing myself together, figuring out myself and what I wanted. And the truth is, I didn't want this. Not now. Maybe not ever.

The thought felt heavy but strangely freeing. I'd been running from it, trying to convince myself that someday, with someone, I'd want to step back into that world of coupledom. But I felt suffocated every time I pictured it— with Sam, with anyone. Like I'd be losing the tiny sliver of peace I'd worked so hard to carve out for myself.

Not to mention, he was my colleague. A man I saw almost daily, whose name was on emails I needed to read, whose decisions I had to trust in a professional setting. The idea of mixing that with romance made my stomach twist. Even if he was a wonderful man, it was a line I didn't want to cross.

For the first time, I let myself really think about what a relationship with Sam would look like. Weekend trips, shared cups of coffee, maybe even dancing to bad pop music in the kitchen. All the things I used to want. And yet, the image felt flat. Like a picture someone else painted and handed to me, insisting it should be my dream.

It was not my dream.

I exhaled slowly.

Sam deserved someone who could give him everything he was looking for. Someone who could meet his kindness with equal measures, who wasn't still fighting ghosts from their past. Someone who wanted what he wanted. And that was not me.

I pushed myself off the door, heading to my desk. I picked up the rose, twirling it between my fingers. Its petals were soft, vibrant, and full of life. A beautiful gesture, but not one I could let take root.

CHAPTER 21: BRUISED HEARTS

The knock on my front door caught me in the middle of a tea sip. I wasn't expecting anyone, so I froze for a moment, debating whether to answer. Then came another knock, this time more insistent. When I opened the door, the sight of Caroline and Linda, both bundled up against the Vermont chill, grinning like they'd just pulled off the heist of the century, caught me.

"Surprise!" Caroline chirped, holding up a grocery bag like a trophy. Linda waved sheepishly, a bottle of wine peeking out from her oversized tote.

"Wait, what—how—what are you doing here?" I stammered, glancing between the two of them.

"People talk," Caroline said with a dramatic wink, brushing past me into the house. "And by 'people,' I meant Sam. He mentioned something about your neighborhood, and we just followed the breadcrumbs."

"You followed breadcrumbs to my house?" I deadpanned, stepping aside to let Linda in.

Linda chuckled as she kicked off her boots. "We thought you could use some company. And some decent food."

"I'm fine," I said, though the warmth spreading through my chest betrayed me. "But thanks for the unsolicited intervention, I guess."

Caroline plopped the grocery bag on my counter, peering around my small but cozy kitchen. "Look at this place! It's like a Pinterest board threw up, but in the best way."

I rolled my eyes, closing the door behind them. "What does that even mean?"

"It means it's cute," she replied, pulling out ingredients and lining them up like she's about to film a cooking show. "And now it's about to smell even cuter. We're making lasagna."

I blinked. "Lasagna?"

Linda set the wine on the counter and shrugged. "Caroline's idea. I'm just here for moral support."

"And to drink wine," Caroline chimed in, handing her a corkscrew with a pointed look.

Caroline clapped her hands, her eyes lighting up like someone had just given her free rein of a gourmet kitchen.

"All right, troops!" she declared, tying a dish towel around her waist like it was a makeshift apron. "Linda, you're on sauce duty. Imara, you're grating cheese. I'll handle the pasta because, well, I trust no one else with boiling water."

"Very gracious of you," I said dryly, grabbing the block of cheese from the counter. "I'm honored to be trusted with such an elite task."

Caroline waved a dismissive hand. "Grate with pride, Hastings. Grate with pride."

Linda rolled her eyes but dutifully moved to the stove, wooden spoon in hand. "I'm stirring the sauce, but if this doesn't taste good, it's on you, Caroline."

"Excuse me," Caroline said, spinning around dramatically. "Everything I touch in the kitchen turns to gold. Or at least edible bronze."

As they bickered, I got to work on the cheese, but it didn't take long before the task evolved into a game. Linda snuck a spoonful of sauce while Caroline was distracted measuring spices, shooting me a mischievous wink when she got away with it.

"You'd think you were starving," I teased, holding up a shred of mozzarella. "Want me to grate this straight into your mouth?"

Linda snorted, but before she could respond, Caroline whirled around. "What's happening here? Are my sous-chefs conspiring against me?"

"Not conspiring," Linda said innocently. "Just quality control."

"Uh-huh," Caroline said, narrowing her eyes as she turned back to the stove. "No one better touch the garlic bread while I'm not looking, or I'm staging a kitchen coup."

By the time the sauce was simmering, and the pasta was boiling, the kitchen smelled like heaven—or what I imagine heaven would smell like if it involved absurd amounts of cheese and garlic. Shreds of mozzarella were all over the counter, some clinging stubbornly to my sweater, and Linda was attempting to sneak another spoonful of sauce behind Caroline's back.

"Linda, step away from the pot," Caroline warned, pointing a salad tong at her like it was a weapon.

Linda raised her hands in mock surrender. "Relax, Gordon Ramsay. It's called taste-testing."

Caroline narrowed her eyes, muttering something about "kitchen betrayal" as she tossed the last of the croutons into the salad. I suppressed a laugh, stacking plates while they bickered.

We migrated to the living room with plates of garlic bread in hand, sinking into the couch as Caroline rifled through the streaming options. She stopped on a Lifetime movie with a title splashed in dramatic red letters across the screen.

"Oh, this one," she said, her eyes lighting up like she'd just uncovered a hidden gem. "It's so bad, it's good."

Linda groaned but didn't argue, and soon, the overly dramatic opening music blared through the room. Within minutes, the plot twists started rolling in: a secret twin! A staged death!—and we were yelling at the screen like it was do anything to change the outcome.

"Of course, she's the twin," Linda said, smirking as the protagonist gasped in slow motion. "It was obvious from the second act."

Caroline threw a pillow at her, missing by a mile. "You're ruining the experience, Linda. Let me enjoy my trash TV in peace."

"It's not trash," I said through a mouthful of garlic bread. "It's... cinematic brilliance."

They both looked at me like I'd grown a second head before we dissolved into laughter, leaning into each other as the movie spiraled further into absurdity.

The morning started unusually perfectly: my coffee was just right—rich and bold, the way I like it. The hospital hummed with a rare kind of calm, the usual chaos simmering down to a manageable buzz. Even Mrs. Carter seemed chipper. She cracked a joke about her oatmeal having the consistency of wallpaper paste, which I countered by suggesting it might double as spackle in an emergency. For once, she laughed instead of rolling her eyes.

Another patient told me I have a "million-dollar smile," and while I knew it was probably just the morphine talking, it was nice to hear.

I spotted Dr. Whitaker lingering near the nurses' station, his eyes scanning the area with a focused intent that instantly put me on edge. I turned sharply on my heel and headed in the opposite direction, suddenly very interested in delivering the extra blanket someone had requested earlier.

"Imara!" His warm and familiar voice carried through the hall, but it made my stomach twist.

I turned reluctantly, plastering on a polite smile. "Dr. Whitaker."

He strode over, his expression easy but his energy unmistakably deliberate. "Do you have a minute? I'd like to talk to you about something."

My heart sank. "Oh, um..." I glanced down at my clipboard, pretending to study it. "Actually, I'm swamped. Could we maybe circle back later?"

He nodded, his smile understanding but persistent. "Of course. Just let me know when you're free."

Sure. Never sounds good, I thought as I forced a tight smile and turned away, clutching my clipboard like a shield. The second I was out of his line of sight, the real game began: Operation Avoid Whitaker.

It was harder than I thought it would be. The man had a knack for appearing at the most inconvenient moments. When I was heading to the break room for a much-needed coffee refill, I spotted him rounding the corner, clipboard in hand.

Without thinking, I pivoted on my heel so fast I almost spilled my empty cup. I mumbled something to Linda, who gave me a confused, perplexed look as I retreated down the hall.

Later, as I was heading to check on a patient, I heard his unmistakable laugh from the nurses' station. My heart jumped, and I darted into the nearest room without looking. Big mistake.

"Oh!" I froze, wide-eyed. The patient—a sweet older gentleman who I'm pretty sure would rather not have visitors right now—was halfway through changing into his hospital gown.

"Sorry! So sorry!" I squeaked, backing out and pulling the door shut behind me. My face burned as I heard a muffled "It's fine!" from inside. I couldn't even bring myself to turn around, knowing I'd probably bump into Sam right outside the door.

By midday, I was a bundle of nerves. Every time I saw him, I found an excuse to slip away. My clipboard became my best friend, a prop to make me look busy as I pretended to be absorbed in invisible tasks. My heart pounded whenever I heard his voice down the hall, and my feet ached from all the detours I'd taken to avoid crossing his path.

By the time the shift wound down, I was mentally and physically exhausted. Caroline noticed as we walked out together, her arm slung over my shoulder in a playful hug.

"You look like you've been through it today," she teased, planting a quick kiss on my cheek. "Go home, get some rest. You deserve it."

I smiled weakly, waving her off as she headed to her car. Relief washed over me as I made my way to mine, ready to collapse into bed and leave the day behind me. But, of course, the universe had other plans.

"Imara."

The sound of my name stopped me in my tracks. I turned slowly, my stomach dropping when I saw him standing by my car, one hand resting casually on the roof.

I stared at him, my heart pounding in my chest. The words "What's up?" barely left my lips when Sam chuckled, the sound low and warm.

"If I didn't know any better," he said, his grin teasing but his eyes steady, "I'd think you've been avoiding me all day."

I forced out a laugh. "Avoiding you? That's ridiculous. I've just been really, really busy today."

"Uh-huh." He raised an eyebrow, clearly unconvinced, but he didn't push it. Instead, he straightened, shoving his hands into his pockets. "Look, I won't keep you long. I just can't go another day without being upfront with you."

My stomach sank. My brain scrambles for an escape route, but there's no way out of this now. "Okay," I said slowly, gripping my car keys a little tighter. "I'm listening."

He took a breath, his gaze unwavering as it locked onto mine. "I'm an honest person, Imara. I like to speak my mind, even when it's not easy. Even when it may not end in my favor, although I have my fingers crossed."

I could feel the heat creeping up my neck. I wanted to stop him, to tell him that this wasn't the time or the place or anything to derail whatever he was about to say. But the words didn't come, and before I could find my footing, he was already stepping off the edge.

"I have feelings for you," he said simply. "In the little time you've been here, I've grown to admire you. You're ambitious and driven, and you care so deeply about your patients. I see the way you connect with them and how you give your all—even when you're tired and hurting. And on top of that…" He hesitated, his eyes flicking away for a brief moment before coming back to mine. "You're beautiful, Imara. And every time you're around, it's like my brain and body forget how to act. I haven't felt that way in years."

His voice dropped, quieter now like he was sharing a secret. "Not since my ex-wife left me. After that, I didn't think I'd ever feel this way about someone again. But then you came along, and suddenly, everything was different. And I can't ignore it anymore. I don't want to."

I stood there, rooted to the spot, unable to form a coherent thought. My mind was spinning, trying to process his words, his tone, the raw sincerity in his eyes.

"I'm not asking for an answer right now," he continued, his voice gentle. "But I wanted to put it out there. I think there's something here, and I'd like to explore it—if you're open to that."

Oh boy. I mean, sure, I was flattered. Who wouldn't be? But also, what?!

My first instinct was to crack a joke. Something like, "Is this the part where you hold up a boombox outside my apartment?" Or maybe, "Are you sure this isn't just the caffeine talking?"

Sam hesitated for a moment, his eyes searching mine as if looking for an opening, some flicker of hope to hold onto. He took a step closer, and I resisted the urge to take one back.

"I don't know what you've been through," he began, his hands still tucked into his pockets as though he was keeping himself from reaching out, "but I do know what it feels like to think love only comes with pain or that it has to be hard to matter and mean anything. I used to think that, too. But it doesn't have to be, Imara. Love can be kind. It can be steady, warm, and easy. I want to show you that."

He was being so open, so vulnerable, and it was almost too much. I looked down at the ground, my brow furrowing as I tried to gather my thoughts. For a moment, I just stared at the gravel underfoot, the cool breeze brushing against my skin.

When I finally lifted my gaze, his face lit up with a flicker of hope. "You don't have to answer right now," he said again, his voice almost eager. "Take your time, Imara. I'll wait."

"Sam..." I began, my voice quiet but steady. "I don't need time to think about it."

His brows furrowed slightly, confusion mingling with the dimming hope in his eyes. "You don't?"

I took a deep breath, forcing myself to meet his gaze even as it felt like the hardest thing I'd done all day. "You're a... great man, Sam. You're patient in ways most people aren't. You listen—not just with your ears, but with your whole self. And you see people, really see them, in a way that makes them feel like they matter. It's through the outreach program, the way you care and look into all possibilities for your patients."

I paused, searching for the right words, my chest tightening. "You bring out the best in people. You make them want to be better. It's incredible."

His lips parted, and for a second, it looked like he was going to speak, but I raised a hand to stop him, a soft, rueful smile tugging at the corners of my mouth. "But that's exactly why I can't do this."

The confusion in his eyes shifted to something deeper— sadness, maybe, or understanding, or some mixture of both. I pressed on before he could respond.

"I'm... not there yet," I admitted. "You said you've had time to heal, and I'm glad you have. But I haven't. And I need that time for myself. I need to figure out who I am and what I want without leaning on someone else to do it for me."

A muscle in his jaw ticked, and his gaze dropped briefly to the floor. When he looked back up, there was a flicker of something raw in his eyes before he smoothed it over with a faint nod. His hands, which had been resting easily in his pockets, curled slightly into fists before relaxing again.

"You deserve someone who's ready, Sam. Someone who can meet you where you are. And right now, that's not me."

He took a small step back, his smile faint but genuine.

"I understand," he said quietly. "I do. And for what it's worth, I think you're doing the right thing."

His words were kind, but they didn't soften the ache in my chest. "Thank you," I murmured, my voice barely above a whisper.

He nodded again, and after a beat of silence, he turned and headed toward his car. I watched as he got in, the taillights glowing faintly as he drove away. Only then did I allow myself to exhale, letting the tension leave my shoulders in a shaky rush.

As the engine hummed softly in the background, I slumped against the steering wheel, a heavy sigh escaping me. The ache in my heart was palpable, but I knew I did the right thing—even if it didn't feel great right now.

I needed a friend, someone who would understand and offer comfort without needing the whole story. I grabbed my phone from the passenger seat and dialed Charlotte's number, pressing it to my ear as it rang.

"Hey," I started, trying to keep my voice steady but failing miserably. "I... could use some company."

There was a brief pause on the other end, and then Charlotte's warm voice filled the silence. "Oh, honey, what's happened? You sound like you've had a day."

I chuckled weakly, brushing a tear from my cheek. "You could say that. It's a long story."

"Say no more," Charlotte interrupted, her tone suddenly brisk and commanding in that comforting way of hers. "Meet me at Sweet Maple. I'm heading there now. You need some of their magic hot cocoa and maybe a giant slice of pie."

The corners of my mouth twitched upwards at her typical directness. "I'll be there in ten," I said, a small spark of gratitude warming the cold dread inside me.

"Make it five."

CHAPTER 22: YOU AGAIN

The soft glow of Sweet Maple's warm lights cut through the chilly Vermont evening as I parked and stepped out of the car. Charlotte was already outside, leaning casually against the wooden railing with her signature scarf tossed over one shoulder. She beamed when she spotted me, arms wide open.

"There's my favorite damsel in distress," she teased, pulling me into a hug. "Come on, let's eat some meat pies and chitchat. You look like you need it."

I chuckled softly, looping my arm through hers as she led me inside. It was not crowded, just a few small groups scattered at tables, the quiet hum of conversation filling the space.

Personal touches were everywhere, sprinkled throughout the café. A mural on one wall depicted a lively street scene with bold patterns and bright colors reminiscent of African art. On the counter, next to the register, was a small sign that read, "Owned with love, inspired by heritage." It's propped up against a delicate wooden carving of a baobab tree.

"Look at that sign. It's practically shaming me for not owning something handmade."

She grinned, nudging me with her elbow. "That's because you've been living in beige apartments your whole life. You're supposed to feel inspired."

"Inspired to what? Whittle a baobab tree out of driftwood?" I muttered, but there was no real heat in my words. The truth was, the café did inspire something—a kind of quiet admiration for whoever had the guts to create a space this unapologetically personal.

Even the menu board had a touch of personality—besides the list of pastries and drinks was a section labeled "Mama's Specials," written in cheerful chalk script. Underneath were items like Jollof Rolls, Coconut Custard Tarts, and other dishes that felt like they came straight from a kitchen filled with laughter and tradition.

"Nice touch, huh?" Charlotte said, noticing my pause. "The owner took over a few months ago. I heard he's got roots in Ghana. It shows."

"It's beautiful," I murmured.

Charlotte nudged me gently. "Wait until you try the meat pies. If they're as good as last time, we'll be ordering seconds."

We headed to the counter to place our order. As Charlotte chatted easily with the barista, I glanced around the café again, taking in the small but thoughtful details. My eyes caught on the kitchen window; the glass fogged slightly from the heat inside.

Through it, I saw a figure—a tall man, his back to me, leaning over a tray of something fresh from the oven. The steam curled around him like a veil, and for a moment, I forgot to blink.

His shoulders were broad, stretching the fabric of his dark shirt, and his posture was relaxed but purposeful, the kind of ease that comes from someone who's deeply at home in what they're doing. His head tilted slightly, revealing a strong, clean jawline before he reached for something off-camera. His movements were fluid, almost hypnotic, and my mind betrayed me with a thought that made my cheeks heat: He's beautiful.

I shook my head slightly, trying to dismiss the ridiculous notion. I couldn't even see his face, for crying out loud. Just a silhouette, a shape that was all angles and grace. But something about him felt familiar. Like I'd seen this figure before, maybe in passing. Maybe in a dream.

Before I could think about it too much, the guilt crept in, as sharp and as sudden as a razor blade cut. "What are you doing?"

My stomach churned, and I took a step back, clutching my coat tighter around me. I just turned someone down, and here I was, shamelessly ogling some stranger through a window.

"Imara, you coming?" Charlotte's voice pulled me from my thoughts. She'd already grabbed our order and was balancing the tray like a pro. Her sharp eyes caught my flustered expression, and she smirked. "What? Did you see a ghost or something?"

"No," I said quickly, clearing my throat. "Just... lost in thought."

"Uh-huh." She didn't buy it but thankfully didn't push. Instead, she looped her arm through mine and dragged me toward a corner booth. "Come on, sit. You look like you've got something to spill."

I let her guide me, glancing back at the kitchen one last time. The man was gone now, and the window was empty. But the image lingered, seared into my mind like an afterimage burned from staring at the sun too long.

Charlotte took a slow sip of her drink as I recounted my day, careful to gloss over most of it but dropping in the key detail: avoiding Dr. Whitaker as my life depended on it.

"He's not a creep, Charlotte. He's just direct. And maybe a little persistent."

Charlotte raised an eyebrow, her skepticism written all over her face. "Persistent is how my neighbor's cat is when it wants food. Persistent doesn't get roses and chocolates involved. You sure he's not crossing a line?"

I hesitated, fiddling with the edge of my napkin. "He's not," I said finally, though the uncertainty in my voice was impossible to miss. "I set my boundary, and he respected it. He hasn't pushed me or made me feel unsafe. It's just complicated."

"Complicated how?"

I exhaled slowly, the words tumbling out before I could stop them. "I hate that I had to turn him down after everything he's been through. The man's wife left him, Charlotte. For someone else. He opened up to me, and then I—"

Charlotte held up a hand, cutting me off. "Imara, stop. Right there." She stared at me, her mouth open in disbelief. "Wait, what? He told you all of this, and then you had to reject him? Are you kidding me?"

Her voice pitched up, and I winced as a few heads turned our way. "Charlotte, shhh! It's not as dramatic as you're making it sound."

She narrowed her eyes, took another sip of her drink, and then shook her head like she couldn't believe what she was hearing. "You've got to be kidding me. The nerve of this man. Who does he think he is, using his heartbreak like some sort of—"

"It wasn't like that!" I cut in, exasperated. "He wasn't trying to guilt me or anything. He was just being honest. He wanted me to know where he was coming from. And I—" I paused, biting my lip. "I just don't know how to feel about it."

Charlotte leaned back, folding her arms across her chest. "I'll tell you how you should feel: like you did the right thing. Because you did."

"Maybe," I murmured, my gaze dropping to my drink. "But it doesn't feel that way. I hate feeling like I hurt him."

"And there's your problem," she said, pointing her straw at me like it was a weapon. "You're always ready to put someone else's needs and feelings before your own. Always trying to make everyone else comfortable, even when it costs you."

Her words hit a little too close to home, and I shifted in my seat uncomfortably. "It's not like I don't care about myself," I said weakly, but even I didn't sound convinced.

She reached across the table and placed her hand over mine. "Caring about yourself doesn't mean ignoring other people. But it does mean setting boundaries and not feeling guilty for protecting your peace. You don't owe anyone a relationship. Not him, not anyone."

I looked up at her, my throat tightening at the sincerity in her eyes. She gently squeezed my hand before pulling back, and I managed a small smile, even as my thoughts remained tangled.

"Thanks, Charlotte," I said quietly.

"Anytime," she replied, picking up her glass again. "Now, enough about Mr. Persistent. Let's focus on the important things—like these meat pies. I'm ordering another round."

CHAPTER 23: PLAYING CUPID

The next morning, I stepped into Mrs. Carter's room with a clipboard in hand and a smile firmly in place. She was sitting upright in bed, her hair styled in its usual neat curls and her knitting needles clicking away at what looked like the beginnings of a scarf.

"I was starting to think you'd forgotten all about little old me."

I laughed, pulling up a chair beside her bed. "Mrs. Carter, I've been here for approximately three seconds, and you're already giving me grief. You sure you're not feeling better than you're letting on?"

She huffed, finally glancing up from her knitting. "Aches and pains, the usual. But the oatmeal was edible today, so I suppose I can't complain too much. Don't get used to the positivity, though. I've got a reputation to uphold."

"Wouldn't dream of it," I replied, flipping through her chart. "Your vitals are holding steady, which is great. And it looks like Dr. Whitaker's adjustment to your meds is doing the trick."

She narrowed her eyes playfully. "Is that why I've been feeling less like a rusty tin man and more like an actual person? Maybe I should send him a thank-you card. Or bake him a cake."

I raised an eyebrow. "You bake?"

She smirked. "I didn't say it'd be edible."

I laughed again, shaking my head as I set the chart down. "Fair enough. So, what are we working on today? Is that a scarf in the works?"

"Could be," she said, holding up the soft, colorful yarn. "Depends on whether my hands cooperate or decide to stage a rebellion halfway through."

"Well, if anyone can win a battle with unruly hands, it's you."

"Flattery will get you nowhere, Ms. Hastings," she said, though her lips twitched with the hint of a smile.

I leaned back slightly, giving her a knowing look. "Oh, I don't know about that. I seem to recall you smiling just now."

"Lies and slander," she deadpanned, resuming her knitting.

I laughed softly, glancing at her chart one more time before setting it aside. "Anything else I can do for you today? Fluff your pillows? Stage an intervention with the kitchen over their oatmeal?"

She paused her knitting, her eyes glinting with mischief. "Well, since you mentioned it... my grandson visited yesterday."

I blinked, caught off guard by the sudden shift. "Oh? How's he doing?"

"He's doing just fine, thank you," she said, her tone turning smug. "But that's not the point. He said I looked amazing. Told me to pass on his thanks to the nurse who got me back to this 'quality.'" She waved a hand, clearly pleased with herself. "And by 'quality,' he meant I'm looking downright fabulous."

I snorted, shaking my head. "Well, I'll take the compliment. Though I'm sure it's more about your natural glow, Mrs. Carter."

She narrowed her eyes, her knitting needles pausing mid-click. "Oh, don't you dare downplay this, Imara. He was very impressed. And between you and me..." Her voice dropped conspiratorially, "He's single. Handsome. Successful."

"Oh, no. No, no, no. Mrs. Carter, don't even think about it."

"Oh, I'm already thinking about it," she replied smugly, resuming her knitting. "You'd be a perfect match."

I laughed nervously, waving my hand in protest. "I think I've had enough of love matches for a lifetime, thank you very much."

She clicked her tongue, her expression turning downright scandalized. "Ridiculous. You're young, brilliant, and far too charming to waste all that on solitude. Trust me, my dear, you've only just begun."

Her words hit me in a way I didn't quite expect; it left me fumbling for a response. Before I could say anything, she winked, smug satisfaction lighting up her face.

"Now, off you go," she said, waving me toward the door with a flick of her wrist. "You've got rounds to do, and I've got knitting to finish."

I chuckled, shaking my head as I stood. "Fine, but you're not giving him my number. I mean it."

She hummed noncommittally, her needles already clicking again. "We'll see."

I stepped out of Mrs. Carter's room with a small smile still lingering on my lips, her words echoing faintly in my mind. Only just begun. I shook my head, amused by her relentless matchmaking spirit.

As I turned down the hallway, my smile faltered. Crap. Dr. Whitaker was heading straight toward me, files in hand and gaze focused ahead. My feet froze mid-step, and for a split second, I considered diving back into Mrs. Carter's room like a coward. But it's too late—he looks up and spots me.

"Good morning," he said, his voice warm but his smile not quite reaching his brown eyes. It was polite, distant, like the practiced pleasantry you offer a stranger at the grocery store.

I opened my mouth to respond, but what came out was more of a sputter. "Good morning... how are—how's everything?"

His brow quirked slightly, but he just nodded. "All good. Busy as always. Have a good day, Imara."

He gave a polite nod and stepped around me, his pace brisk as he headed down the hall. I glanced back at him, guilt pinching at the edges of my thoughts. He was respecting my boundaries—exactly what I wanted—and yet I couldn't shake the pang of regret that settled in my chest.

I sighed, shaking my head as I kept walking. It'll feel natural eventually. Right?

"Why the long face, Hastings?"

I yelped as Caroline looped her arm through mine from behind, her voice bright and full of mischief. She was grinning like she'd caught me doing something I shouldn't, and I glared at her half-heartedly.

"Don't do that," I said, pressing a hand to my chest. "You scared me."

"Pfft," she scoffed, waving me off. "You were too busy staring off into space to notice me. And what's this?" She waggled her eyebrows dramatically. "Is it the good doctor? Hmm?"

"Don't start," I groaned, trying to wriggle free, but she tightened her grip with a laugh.

"Alright, alright. I'll stop." She was clearly lying, but her grin softened into something more genuine.

"I had an idea while I was reorganizing my crystals."

I raised an eyebrow. "Please tell me this doesn't involve sage or manifesting something weird."

"Excuse me, Hastings," she said, her free hand flying to her chest in faux offense. "Sage is sacred, and manifesting is not weird." She paused for dramatic effect. "But no, it's nothing like that.

I was wondering if you would ever consider hosting one of those classic Vermont dinners. Cozy vibes, comfort food, the whole shebang? You know, lean into the small-town charm and all."

"Me? Host a dinner?"

"Why not?" she said with a shrug. "You've got that cute little apartment, your Southern charm, and now a bunch of locals who actually like you. Why not?"

The idea settled in my mind, surprising me with how appealing it sounded. I'd never considered myself a host, but... maybe it could be nice.

"I'll think about it," I said cautiously, earning Caroline's triumphant grin.

Caroline was still looping her arm through mine as Linda fell into step on my other side, her clipboard tucked under her arm.

"Look at this," she teased, her tone mock-serious. "The hospital's golden child, walking these halls like she owns the place."

I groaned, rolling my eyes. "I'm not a 'golden child.' I just do my job."

"Sure, sure," Linda said, grinning. "That's exactly what a 'gold star' nurse would say."

Caroline snickered. "Gold star, huh? You hear that, Imara? Better get that embroidered on your scrubs."

"Or tattooed on my forehead," I deadpanned, earning laughs from both of them.

Linda nudged me with her elbow. "Jokes aside, you fit in pretty well around here. So, tell us—any chance you're thinking of sticking around in Vermont for good?"

The question caught me off guard, but I recovered quickly, shooting her a wry smile. "Me? Settling down in Vermont? You're funny, Linda. I didn't realize comedy was part of your job description."

Caroline let out a dramatic sigh. "She's avoiding the question."

"Completely."

I shrugged, keeping my expression light. "I'll tell you what— when I figure out what I'm doing with my life, you two will be the first to know."

As I settled into my bed, the soft glow of my bedside lamp casting a warm circle of light, my phone buzzed on the nightstand. I glanced at the screen and smiled. Mama Bear.

Swiping to answer, I brought the phone to my ear. "Hey, Mama."

"Hey, baby girl," she said. "How are you holding up? You eat, right?"

I chuckled, leaning back against the headboard. "Yes, Mama. I even cooked the other night—well, with a little help. Caroline and Linda came over."

"That's good," she said, but I could hear the pause in her voice, the unspoken concern she was too proud to voice outright. "Your daddy wanted me to ask if you're taking your vitamins."

"Daddy?" I laughed. "Since when does he care about vitamins? I thought he was more into vitamin D—Dominos."

"Oh, he's out playing dominos right now," she said with a huff. "Acting like he doesn't have work to do around here."

Her exasperation made me smile. "Tell him I said hi when he gets back. And to take it easy on the poor souls he's beating out there."

She snorted, but her tone softened. "I will. And don't you let those nurses overwork you up there. You sound tired."

"I'm fine, mom," I assured her, swinging my legs over the side of the bed. The gentle sway of my feet feels grounding. "Things are... good. Busy, but good."

"You sure?" She pressed, her voice dropping just enough to remind me that she could read me like a book, even over the phone.

I hesitated, but only for a moment. "Yeah, Mama. I'm sure."

She let out a small sigh, and I imagined her sitting at the kitchen table, probably with a glass of sweet tea and the family Bible open in front of her. "Well, just remember, you don't have to do everything alone. We're always here, you know that."

"I know. Thanks, Mama."

"Oh, and before I forget—you won't believe what happened."

"What?" I asked cautiously, sensing the buildup.

"Your friend Tania and that boy Derek had an explosive argument in the middle of the grocery store. I mean, full-on shouting, breaking eggs, the whole nine yards."

I blinked, stunned for a brief moment, before a laugh busted out of me. "Breaking eggs? Are you serious?"

"Oh, dead serious," she replied, her laugh joining mine. "It was a scene, Imara. A scene. People are still talking about it."

I shook my head, torn between disbelief and amusement. "I... I don't even know what to say. What were they even arguing about?"

"Who knows with those two," she said dismissively. "All I know is, it's a good thing you're not here to get dragged into that mess."

"No kidding," I murmured, relief washing over me.

"I just hope they figure it out," I added, my voice softer now. "For their own sake."

There was a pause, and then my mother said, "I'm proud of you, baby."

The words caught me off guard, and my breath hitched slightly. "For what?"

"For getting out. For taking care of yourself," she said firmly. "You've been through a lot, and you still made something more of yourself: you ventured to places even I've never dreamed of being. That's something to be proud of."

I wasn't sure you'd feel that way," I admitted quietly. "At first, I thought... you'd be upset."

She let out a soft sigh, the kind she used when she was trying to find the right words. "Of course, I was hesitant at first. Angry. What mother wouldn't be? Watching my baby pack up and move halfway across the country—especially after everything... it wasn't easy."

Her voice wavered slightly; it was the closest thing to raw emotion I'd ever heard from her. "But I also knew you needed this. To find yourself, to heal. And if Vermont is where you needed to be to do that, then how could I continue to stand in your way?"

I bit the inside of my cheek. "I miss you guys," I whispered, my voice cracking.

"We miss you too," she said softly. "Every day. But you're doing exactly what you need to do, and that's what matters."

"Thanks, Mama. That means a lot."

"It's the truth," she said gently. "Now, you get some rest, alright? And don't let anything or anyone steal your peace."

"I won't," I promised, and this time, I truly meant it.

CHAPTER 24: GIRLFRIENDS

By the time Saturday morning rolled around, I was standing in my kitchen, staring at an empty notepad with a pen poised over it. A "classic Vermont dinner" sounded charming when Caroline suggested it. Now, it just sounded like an invitation to embarrass myself.

The knock at my door was brisk, and when I opened it, Caroline and Linda were standing there, armed with reusable bags and matching mischievous grins.

"All right, Chef Hastings," Caroline said, brushing past me like she owned the place. "Let's talk strategy."

"Or lack thereof," Linda quipped, dropping her bag on the counter. "We heard you can barely boil water without supervision."

I crossed my arms, aiming for a dignified look that probably came off more pouty. "I can cook."

Linda raised an eyebrow. "Define 'cook.'"

"Define 'barely boil water,'" I shot back, and Caroline let out a billowy laugh as she rifled through the nearest bag.

"Relax, Imara. We're here to make sure you don't accidentally poison anyone," Caroline said, pulling out a small jar of maple syrup with a dramatic flourish. "First rule of Vermont cooking: this goes on everything."

I rolled my eyes but couldn't fight the smile tugging at my lips. "So, you're saying pancakes for dinner?"

"Only if you're trying to lose friends," Linda said dryly, already jotting something down on the notepad. "How about roast chicken? Or a pot roast? That's safe."

Caroline gasped in mock horror. "Safe? We don't do safe. We do memorable."

"You're doing dinner, not hosting a circus," Linda fired back, and I sank onto a stool, letting them bicker as I sipped my coffee.

Another knock broke up their debate, and I hopped off the stool, already expecting it. "That'll be Charlotte."

Linda shot me a look. "You called for reinforcements?"

"More like I needed a buffer," I replied, yanking the door open to find Charlotte standing there, looking like she belonged on the cover of a lifestyle magazine.

"Good lord," she said, stepping into the kitchen uninvited. Her sharp eyes scanned the chaos of bags and ingredients on my counters. "This is what you're working with? We've got our work cut out for us."

"Charlotte!" I folded my hands in mock reverence. "Please save me."

Caroline and Linda exchanged looks before Caroline stepped forward, her curiosity practically radiating off her. "Who is this Vermont version of you, Imara?"

"Oh, where are my manners?" I said, gesturing between them. "Charlotte, meet Caroline and Linda. Caroline and Linda meet Charlotte. She's a friend I met at the boot store near the pharmacy, and she's here to make sure I don't burn my house down."

"Friend is a strong word," Charlotte said dryly, but the corners of her lips twitched upward. "I'm more of a benevolent savior."

Caroline gasped, her eyes lighting up. "Wait! Is she the one who helped you get rid of those hideous boots?"

"Those weren't boots," Charlotte cut in dryly, crossing her arms. "They were clown shoes in disguise."

I groaned, waving them off. "Okay, okay, let's all remember who's actually hosting this dinner. And for the record, I didn't buy the boots."

"Because I stopped you," Charlotte said with a mockingly stern look. "You're welcome."

Caroline grinned. "I like her already."

Linda narrowed her eyes. "Are you any good in the kitchen, or are you here for moral support?"

Charlotte raised an eyebrow, unimpressed. "Sweetheart, I've forgotten more about cooking than you'll ever know. And moral support? Not my style."

The room went silent for a beat before Caroline let out a bark of laughter, clapping her hands. "Oh, you're going to fit in just fine."

Linda cracked a grin, finally relenting. "Alright, show us what you've got, Chef Charlotte."

Charlotte smirked, setting her tin box and herbs on the counter. "Let's start with not ruining whatever you've planned so far."

"I resent that!" Caroline protested, but she was smiling. "We've got solid ideas. Roast chicken with maple glaze, cheddar biscuits—"

"And pie!" Linda added quickly, pointing a pen at Charlotte like she was issuing a challenge.

Charlotte sniffed, unimpressed. "Not bad. But if we're doing pie, it needs to have a proper crust. None of that store-bought nonsense."

"Agreed," Linda said, finally warming up to Charlotte. "You think you can pull it off, Imara?"

"Excuse me," I said, glaring at all three of them. "I'm standing right here. And yes, I can pull it off. Probably."

Caroline looped an arm around my shoulders, grinning. "Don't worry. We've got you."

Charlotte looked between them and then at me. "You weren't kidding. They're not half bad."

As the laughter died down, I grabbed a notepad from the counter and slapped it in the middle of the table. "Alright, if we're doing this, we're doing it right. Let's get organized before this turns into chaos."

"Organized? You?" Charlotte smirked, leaning back in her chair. "This should be good."

I rolled my eyes. "Hush. You're already on thin ice."

She waved me off like she couldn't care less. "Fine, I'll take decor. Someone needs to make sure this dinner doesn't look like a middle school bake sale." She paused, then added,

"Don't worry. I'll keep it tasteful. None of those tacky seasonal gourds."

Caroline gasped, clutching her chest dramatically. "Tacky? Gourds are quintessential Vermont!"

Charlotte raised an eyebrow, her tone dry. "Not when they're spray-painted gold and glittered like a Vegas showgirl."

Caroline snickered but didn't argue. "Fair point. Fine, you're on decor duty."

"Glad we agree," Charlotte said, already jotting it down in the notepad like she was the CEO of this operation.

Linda scrolled through her phone, her face serious. "I'll handle the memories. Someone's gotta hunt down a decent digital camera so we can document this for posterity."

"Digital camera?" Caroline stared at her. "What is this, 2003?"

"Laugh all you want," Linda said, holding up her phone. "But when you see these blurry photos versus the high-res masterpiece I create, you'll eat your words."

Caroline shook her head. "I'm not sure what's worse: your camera obsession or the fact that you still say 'high-res.'"

Ignoring her, Linda added her task to the list with a flourish.

I sipped my coffee, suppressing a laugh. "Alright, what about groceries?"

Caroline perked up. "That's us, obviously. You and me, grocery store warriors. I'll teach you the sacred art of coupon hunting. It's a life skill, Imara."

"Coupon hunting?" I arched an eyebrow. "What is this, 1999?"

"Mock me now," she said, pointing a finger at me. "But you'll thank me later when you save $5 on maple syrup."

"I'll believe it when I see it," I muttered, shaking my head.

Charlotte looked between us, muttering under her breath. "I can't believe I'm friends with you people."

"Oh, you love us," Linda quipped, her grin wide. Charlotte didn't respond, but the faintest smile tugged at her lips.

"Sunday it is," I said, scribbling the date at the top of the notepad. "Let's just hope my house survives this."

"With us on your team?" Caroline said, clinking her coffee mug against mine. "What could possibly go wrong?"

A lot, I thought, but I kept it to myself. As I looked around the table at my mismatched group of friends, I felt something warm bloom in my chest—excitement. This might actually be fun.

CHAPTER 25: CINNAMON

The grocery store was bustling, the faint hum of chatter mixing with the clatter of carts against tiled floors. Caroline pushed the cart ahead of me; every few minutes, she would pull out her phone and scroll quickly before shoving it back into her pocket. It was subtle, but by the third time, I couldn't ignore it.

"So," I said, grabbing a jar of marinara from the shelf and tossing it into the cart. "You've been unusually quiet today. And don't think I haven't noticed all the phone-checking. What's up?"

She froze mid-air while reaching for a jar of Alfredo sauce, her lips pressing into a tight line. "What? Nothing. I'm just... multitasking."

I raised an eyebrow, crossing my arms. "Multitasking, huh? By staring at your phone like it owes you money?"

Caroline huffed out a laugh, shaking her head. "Fine. You caught me. It's—ugh, it's stupid."

"Stupid?" I echoed, nudging the cart forward. "You're practically radiating stress over there. Spill."

She hesitated, her fingers hovering over a jar of alfredo. "There's this guy," she said finally, her tone nonchalant, even though her cheeks betrayed her with the faintest hint of pink.

I stopped mid-step, my interest piqued. "A guy?"

"Yes, a guy," she said, rolling her eyes as she tossed the jar into the cart. "But don't get excited. It's nothing serious. I haven't even told Linda or Charlotte about it yet."

I nudged her playfully. "Well, I'm honored. What's he like?"

"Cute. Funny. Good cook. But," she paused, looking conflicted, "I don't know. It's still so early, and I'm not sure if I should even be putting myself out there right now."

I nodded, grabbing a pack of brown sugar. "Fair. But you deserve to have fun. Just... be careful, okay?"

She smiled, her gaze softening. "Look at you, all-wise and protective. You need to take your advice, though."

I scoffed, waving her off. "We're not talking about me."

"Oh, we absolutely are," she retorted, grinning. "You've got this 'I'm sworn off love forever' vibe going, but don't think I haven't noticed the way you're starting to soften up around people."

Before I could protest, she pointed toward the spice aisle. "Go grab some cinnamon. I'll meet you by the dairy section."

Grateful for the escape, I headed down the aisle, scanning the shelves for the elusive bottle of cinnamon. My eyes locked onto the last one, tucked on the top shelf. Just as I stretched for it, another hand reached out for it at the same moment.

We froze, my fingers brushing the glass bottle as I looked up—straight into the piercing gaze of a tall, broad-shouldered man. For a split second, my brain stuttered. His sharp features were unmistakable, from his strong jawline to the faint furrow of his brows.

The store—oh, the store. The unapologetic bump that nearly sent me into a rack of overpriced muffins, his back already turned before I could gather the breath to say anything. The man who managed to irritate me in under five seconds flat and vanish just as quickly.

The bar. A fleeting glimpse of him at Sweet Maple, slipping into the kitchen. The faint scent of cologne lingered in the narrow hallway as he passed by, brushing my shoulder without so much as a backward glance.

"You," I said, pointing a finger at him before I could stop myself, the irritation in my voice clear.

His dark brows drew together, his expression shifting to cautious confusion. "Excuse me?"

"You're the guy—" I started, but then I realized how ridiculous I sounded. "Never mind."

He didn't drop it, of course. "The guy who... what?"

I huffed, reaching for the cinnamon on the shelf. Before I could grab it, his hand darted out and snatched it, his movements quick and precise. He held the bottle up like it was a prize.

"I need this more than you do," he said, his voice deep and matter-of-fact, like he was declaring a law of nature.

"Excuse me?" My eyes narrowed, and I crossed my arms over my chest.

"You heard me," he replied, giving a nonchalant shrug. "It's for my café. Cinnamon rolls. Best in town."

I let out a short laugh, the disbelief audible. "Right. Because your cinnamon rolls are more important than my dinner party."

"Absolutely," he said, his tone infuriatingly calm. "The café's a staple of the community. People rely on us. Tourists flock to us."

"Oh, well then," I said, gesturing dramatically toward the bottle in his hand. "By all means, take it. We wouldn't want to deprive the masses of their cinnamon roll fix."

He smirked, the corner of his mouth twitching up. "I appreciate your selflessness."

"Not so fast." I grabbed the edge of the bottle, trying to tug it from his grip, but he didn't let go.

"How many rolls are we talking about here?" I asked, narrowing my eyes. "Because I'm feeding a whole party of newcomers who are counting on me to prove that I've got this Vermont thing figured out."

He blinked, caught slightly off guard. "How many people?"

"Enough to warrant cinnamon," I said firmly, tugging harder on the bottle.

"Cute," he said, his grip tightening. "But I'm serving a café full of locals and out-of-towners. Cinnamon rolls are practically a breakfast rite of passage. You really want to be responsible for disappointing them?"

"Oh, please," I shot back. "They'll survive one day without your famous rolls."

"Will they?" he countered, his voice dropping just slightly like he was sharing some deep philosophical truth.

I paused, my grip loosening for just a second. "Look," I said, switching tactics. I'm new in town. This dinner party is my chance to make an impression. I'm trying to fit in here."

His smirk barely softened, but he didn't let go of the cinnamon. "You want to fit in? Easy. Serve apple pie. Or maple something. They'll love you."

"I already have apples and maple covered," I replied, tugging on the bottle again. "And I need the cinnamon to finish it. So, if you don't mind—"

"Excuse me," an older woman said, interrupting as she reached for a bottle of nutmeg beside us. The moment broke, and I stepped back, biting my tongue as he turned to leave with the cinnamon still in his hand.

For a second, I told myself to let it go. It was just cinnamon. There was probably another bottle somewhere else in the store.

But then I thought about how he bumped into me so rudely that day at Sweet Maple, and now he was walking away like he owned the spice aisle.

Not a chance.

"Hey!" I called, already weaving through the crowd to catch up with him. He was taller than everyone else in the aisle, which made him easy to spot as he rounded the corner. "Wait a minute!"

He stopped and turned, his expression a mix of annoyance and disbelief. "Are you seriously chasing me over cinnamon?"

"Yes," I said without hesitation, stopping just short of bumping into him. "First, you nearly knock me over without so much as an apology. Now, you're stealing cinnamon right out of my grasp. What's next? My cart?"

He blinked at me, clearly taken aback, but the corner of his mouth twitched like he was holding back a laugh. "Stealing? I picked it up first."

"No, I touched it first. You snatched it." I crossed my arms, staring him down. "There's a difference."

"Is there?" he countered, lifting the bottle like it was some kind of holy grail. "I didn't realize cinnamon was such a hot commodity."

I could feel my temper rising, but instead of snapping, I let out an incredulous laugh. "You know, this is kind of funny."

He raised an eyebrow. "Oh, yeah? How so?"

I shook my head, my laugh turning into something closer to a giggle. "You, me, and this cinnamon. It's like a low-budget reenactment of my ex and his girlfriend fighting over eggs in the middle of a grocery store."

His brow furrowed, and he stared at me like I'd grown a second head. "I'm sorry—what?"

"Never mind." I waved him off, still laughing. "You can't just walk through life—bumping into people, hoarding spices, acting like you're entitled to whatever you want. That's not how it works."

His smirk widened, and he leaned casually against the nearest shelf, clearly enjoying this far too much. "Wow. You've got me all figured out, huh?"

"Pretty much," I shot back, refusing to back down.

For a moment, I thought he was going to walk away, but then he sighed and extended it toward me. "Fine. Take it. There are other stores."

"Thank you," I said, grabbing it triumphantly. "See? Was that so hard?"

His gaze lingered on me for a second longer than necessary, and there was something unreadable in his expression. Then, without another word, he turned and walked away, his tall frame cutting through the crowded aisle like he didn't have a care in the world.

I clutched the cinnamon, a small pang of something—guilt? Sadness?—settling in my chest as I watched him go. For all his smugness, something about his demeanor felt... familiar. Shaking my head, I pushed the thought aside and headed back to find Caroline.

"Well," I muttered under my breath, glancing at the cinnamon in my hand. "At least I won."

Back at the spice aisle, Caroline raised an eyebrow as I dropped the cinnamon triumphantly into the cart. "Did I just see you arguing with Mrs. Carter's grandson?"

I froze mid-motion, staring at her. "What?"

She nodded, crossing her arms with a knowing smirk. "Yeah, that was Noah. You didn't know?"

"No, I didn't know," I muttered, my voice rising an octave.

"Oh, that's rich," Caroline said, laughing as she tossed a box of pasta into the cart. "You mean to tell me you've been sparring with the guy your favorite patient has been trying to set you up with for weeks?"

I groaned, pressing a hand to my forehead. "Wait—he's the grandson? The one she's always going on about? Successful, charming, oh-so-handsome?"

"That's the one," she said, grinning like she'd just been handed front-row seats to the drama of the year. "Though technically, he's adopted. But she treats him like her golden child."

Suddenly, it all clicked—the wit, the sarcasm, the way he carried himself like he owned the room. "Oh, it makes sense now. The attitude? Totally a family trait."

Caroline cackled, nudging me with her elbow. "Well, at least we know he's got good genes. And you two seemed to be... connecting."

"'Connecting' is one way to put it," I muttered, gripping the cart a little tighter as I steered us toward the next aisle. "I was about two seconds away from shoving him into a display of nutmeg."

At home, I moved around the kitchen, unpacking groceries and lining up jars and cans with an almost obsessive precision. In its own, unique way, filling the quiet with the rustling of paper bags and the soft thud of boxes finding their place on the shelves was comforting. But no matter how much I tried to focus on the task, my mind kept circling back to him.

Noah.

Why did he have to look like that? Like someone took all the charm and confidence in the world and wrapped it up in broad shoulders and a jawline that could probably crack walnuts. His eyes were sharp and intense, like he could see right through me, which was both annoying and... distracting. And the way he leaned on that cart? Like the whole aisle revolved around him, it wasn't fair, really. No one should look that good while stealing cinnamon.

I shoved a jar of pasta sauce onto the shelf a little harder than necessary and exhaled sharply. "Cinnamon," I shook my head. Of all the things to argue about.

Who was this man, and why did every encounter with him feel like a page out of a book I didn't remember reading or writing?

I caught myself smiling as I closed the fridge and pressed my back against it, the coolness of the door a grounding contrast to the warmth spreading through my chest. "Get it together, Imara," I muttered, brushing a strand of hair from my face. "It's not that deep."

Still, the image of him turning to leave—broad shoulders, confident stride, the faintest hint of amusement lingering in his expression—stuck with me. For someone so annoying, he carried himself with an ease that was... compelling. And that smirk. It wasn't just confident; it was infuriatingly self-assured, like the smirk of a man who knew exactly how to get under my skin specifically.

My phone rang, snapping me out of my thoughts. I glanced at the screen, expecting Charlotte or Caroline, but the name that lit up the display sent my heart plummeting.

CHAPTER 26: NOAH

"Derek."

There was silence on the other end—just a faint crackle of air—and for a second, I thought maybe he'd hung up. But then his voice came through, low and hesitant. "Imara."

What caught me off guard was how he said my name, like it still belonged to him or as if he had the right to pull me back into his orbit. I let the silence stretch, hoping he'd feel the weight of all the months that had passed without a single word from him.

"I didn't think you'd pick up," he said finally, his voice edging toward something... softer. "But I've been thinking, and I needed to call."

"Thinking?" I echoed, my tone flat. "Derek, it's been months. What could you possibly have to think about?"

He exhaled sharply like he was gearing up for a speech. "I heard you left the state. That you're... gone. I—I just didn't expect that. You didn't even tell me."

I snorted softly, leaning against the counter. "Yeah, Derek, that's generally what happens when someone cheats on you with your best friend. They don't send a postcard when they move on."

His silence was long this time, and for a second, I almost felt bad: almost! But then he spoke, his voice quieter, like he was trying to tiptoe around the shards of the mess he made. "Look, I know I messed up, okay? I know I hurt you, and I hate myself for it. But... I haven't stopped thinking about you, Imara."

My grip tightened on the phone, my chest twisting in a way I'm not entirely proud of. "Derek, what do you want? Why are you calling me?"

"To talk," he said, his tone soft but unsure, like even he didn't believe his own excuse. "To explain."

"Explain?" I let out a sharp laugh, the bitterness bleeding through. "You're engaged, Derek. What explanation could possibly make a difference now?"

There was a long pause, and when he spoke again, his voice cracked just enough to catch me off guard. "I thought I was doing the right thing, trying to move on. But I can't. I haven't. I thought... maybe you felt the same."

I froze, his words hitting like a cold wind. "Are you kidding me?" I asked, my voice sharper now. "You don't get to rewrite history just because you're feeling lonely, Derek. You made your choice."

"Imara, please," he said, desperation creeping into his tone. "I know I'm the last person you want to hear from. I know I don't deserve another chance, but I—" His voice broke, and I could practically hear him running a hand through his hair, just like he always did when he was spiraling. "I don't know how to let you go."

I closed my eyes, the weight of his words pressing down on me. A part of me wanted to scream at him and tell him exactly how much damage he'd done. But there was another part—smaller, quieter—that just wanted to hang up and move on without giving him the satisfaction of knowing he still had any effect on me.

"Derek," I said finally, my tone steady, cold. "You already did." And before he could respond, I hung up.

The kitchen was a mess, but it was the kind of mess that made me smile instead of cringe. Ingredients were all over the counter: fresh herbs in mismatched bowls, a bag of flour with a tear spilling onto the wood grain, and bottles of wine lined up like soldiers ready for duty.

My friends' handwriting was scrawled across the recipe cards pinned to the fridge with mismatched magnets. Every corner of the room was alive with signs of them—Charlotte's forgotten scarf draped over a chair, Linda's half-empty wine glass near the sink, and Caroline's overly detailed grocery list crumpled on the table.

This is what I needed.

I ran a finger along the edge of the counter, tracing a faint flour streak left behind from Charlotte's ambitious pie crust.

It was messy, but it was mine. It was mine because they made it for me. Because somehow, without me realizing it, I'd found a little corner of the world where I fit and felt wanted and needed.

The thought tightened my throat, but I swallowed it down, a small smile tugging at my lips. This is what it felt like, isn't it? To belong. To be part of something that's not perfect but still whole.

As I cleaned up the kitchen, a buzz from my phone drew my attention. A new message from an unknown number.

Unknown: *"I'm texting under duress. My aunt insisted. Something about a cane, and I don't feel like testing her resolve."*

I frowned, wiping my hands on a dish towel before unlocking my phone.

Me: *"Uh, wrong number?"*

The reply was almost instant.

Unknown: *"Oh, no. This is exactly the right number, trust me. She gave it to me and said I "owed it to her favorite nurse."*

I stared at the screen, the pieces slowly clicking into place. Just as I was about to reply, another message popped up.

Unknown: *"It's Noah. Cinnamon aisle. Sweet Maple kitchen. Eternal thorn in your side? Ring any bells?"*

A laugh escaped me before I could stop it. Of course. Mrs. Carter.

Me: *"You're telling me she gave you my number?"*

Noah: *"Let's just say she's persuasive. And by persuasive, I mean terrifying when armed with a cane and a mission."*

I snorted, shaking my head.

Me: *"So you're only texting me to avoid potential injury?"*

Noah: *"Absolutely. I'm here under protest. However, I do feel obligated to remind you that I let you win the cinnamon battle out of kindness."*

Me: "*You didn't let me win. I earned that cinnamon fair and square, and we both know it.*"

Noah: "*Debatable. But if I'm going to be blackmailed into texting you, I might as well offer some advice: Your first Vermont dinner party? Go heavy on the maple. People eat that up—literally.*"

I grinned, glancing at the bags of groceries scattered across the counter.

Me: "*Don't tell me you're the party-planning type.*"

Noah: "*I'm not. But I do know how to keep people happy. You can thank me later when they're singing your praises.*"

Me: "*You're assuming I'll take your advice.*"

Noah: "*You'd be foolish not to. But I'm guessing you're stubborn enough to ignore me anyway.*"

I chuckled, leaning back against the counter. His tone practically leaped off the screen—dry, confident, and just cocky enough to be infuriating. And yet... I found myself typing back.

Me: *"I'll let you know if your advice works. And if it doesn't, you'll be the one explaining to Mrs. Carter why I ruined dinner."*

Noah: *"Deal. Though you should know, I'm excellent at deflecting blame, Imara. Comes with the territory."*

I froze, rereading the message. My name. He used my name.

Heat rushed to my cheeks before I could stop it, a blush creeping its way across my face like it owned the place. My stomach did an involuntary flip, and I hated the fact that it was happening—absolutely hated it.

It's just a name. My name. Nothing special. Nothing worth reacting to.

And yet, here I was, staring at the screen like a lovesick teenager.

With a shake of my head, I locked my phone and set it on the counter, determined not to let his words—or the way they made me feel—get the better of me. Not tonight.

But as I glanced at the bags of groceries and the small chaos in my kitchen, I couldn't help the faint smile that tugged at my lips. Vermont just got a whole lot more interesting.

Continue the journey.

Get sneak peeks, bonus scenes, and early access to new releases.

👉 Tap here: https://subscribepage.io/foS9zc

🔳 Or scan the QR code below:

THE END